The Thought Experiment

Something to do with nothing to learn

By

Marshall Sanders

Introduction

First off I would like to thank all my friends who believed in my chaotic mind. I would like to thank my Faith; I'll never lose my Lady Faith.

There are some miss-phrases and typos, but I'm a writer not an editor, but the stories are there. Remember though that is what they are, just stories. Anything that seems real is just a coincidence, I'm sorry but you're not worth writing about and neither am I. Life is worth writing about though, so I apologize once again if there are any similarity's.

This is a small collection of short stories and poems I typed up while exploring Western Europe. I am sorry for not numbering the pages. I hope that this collection catches your interest enough to read through. I believe you'll find and enjoy the diversity which lies within. The truth in these stories are only known and noticeable by me. I never want to offend anybody but myself. Please read

and enjoy and I hope you can build a
relation with what is not being said.
Through all my publications and
writings I feel that they focus simply
on the complex issues we all as
individuals face daily. Thank You Very
Much for taking the time to read this
collection. Good Luck in this rat race

Marshall Sanders

Contents

The pages that follow. I kid
I hope you pick it up and don't
put it down and see the diversity

Sweet sleep

I take a few minutes from writing to look at her. She is a sleep on my bed. It's a bit chilly, so I get up and turn the heat up for her. She looks so relaxed, like she is able to forget life for awhile. Maybe it's because she is forgetting me? I want her to know how much I love her, but she is a better person than me, I have become a lost cause. For that reason we both know that I am not made for her. I enjoy our current chapter in life together and believe that she might be to.

Smoking, drinking, was rolling up to many joints at 3am while she sleeps sweetly. I always had fresh washed sheets and a quilt down for her. I do this because she wraps herself in them as she is right now while I look at her. I wondered if I could ever sleep relaxed like that and show it, but for some reason I doubted this. To many nights I awake to a lockjaw or leg and back spasms and the dreaded vomiting. She never has this problem, I imagine she sleeps long enough to dream sweet dreams, or attempt to. I envy this. I envy this, but enjoy and find it peaceful watching her sleep. My record player plays softly in the background, never loud enough to bother her. The music starts to calm my mind, my body.

I find myself just wanting to listen to the music, drink and just watch her beautiful body rest. The morning has passed fast though and I am growing tired. She has been laying the same way for the last couple of hours, but I decided to lie next to her.

Maybe I won't think long enough to fall asleep, to have that deep, sweet sleep. So I wrap her in my arms.

2AM cigarette burns

Laying awake, already dreading the thought of work. I get up and decide to have a beer. I turn on the TV and there is nothing on, thought it might bore me to sleep, but I've never been able to sleep with the TV on for some reason. I turn the TV off and turn on the record player. I decided to write. I light a joint and begin to write. I write about everything that comes to my hazy mind.

The music helps my mind flow. I keep drinking and smoke too many cigarettes. The words where flowing like the beer. I start to get bored. The music takes over, along with the booze. I get up to get my acoustic and look around. I see a small room with pictures all over the wall, a bunch of maps of Europe, to many beer cans and an ashtray full of butts. I look down at the rug that I put under my desk for this very reason, there were about ten new cigarette burns. I love those early morning highs, listening to music, and writing. I had to change and go to work

A moment to
Wonder

Depression has set in once again.
Doesn't it seem odd, that in a world so full
of so many people, that you could still feel
alone? So alone sitting in a one bedroom
apartment, wondering if I stepped outside
would I actually see life, or would I just
get disappointed in the cheap imitation?
    To get out of bed would only depress me
further. I don't want to lead myself to
tears as the truth of the world seeps into
my soul. The thought doesn't scare me, the
thought just takes my hours and turns them
to months, and time is the scariest of all.
I see some soul sometimes that I use to
know, wondering if they are happy, or if it
is the smile that makes me wonder.
    I sit on this early, early morning hour
doing just that, wondering. I try to make
myself not wonder, but I can't help but do
just that. I wonder about Tanya the girl I
had a crush on at a young age, after seeing
her for the first time in years, I wonder.
Does she spare a thought for me, or was her
hug a natural movement. I wonder about a lot
of the girls at that gathering, having a
history with some and moments with others.
Did I suck the soul from these innocent
girls at one point? I know that I am not
worthy or capable of such a thing, but did
they despise me, was this the reason for my
staying in bed. Countless hours of trying to
accomplish life and being scared to move,

becoming a coward for reasons unknown.

    I did not know, but now I didn't care anymore. Just like that I know that some people were fucked from the beginning and others are lucky. I think suddenly that this was all just a bad thought, probably stupid to think too much into.

Alcohol, the cause of life's problems and the answer

I blacked out again. This was the third time I have blacked out this week. I sit in my empty house, to scared to leave. It seems too many people are out to get me, or want something from me, for me to do something for them. I could really care less. I grab my handle of vodka and let my dog out to use the restroom. My poor dog has to sit in silence with me due to my condition.

"Don't drink, don't smoke, eat healthier," this was what I was hearing all the time. "You're only making it worse." I think about my life. I'm not an old man, middle aged, still good looking. I no longer can play my guitar though, it wears me out, I can barely write.

I think about my ex-wife and the problems I caused between us. I never

hit her though, but nonetheless I was
an angry drunk. Heather took it good
for about a year before leaving me. My
dog was the only thing that hasn't
given up on me, but it is pointless as
I wait my turn to die. I drink and
smoke to forget. I want to forget so
much.

    December is ending and fucks with
me as the New Year is not well
receipted, but I can't keep it from
running its course. I take a swig from
my vodka and chase it down thinking of
all the great times, not of my death
though. The innocent never made it this
far, only the strong and stupid. I
black out again and wake in the early
morning hours. I was okay with this.
It meant I could forget about life for
a while. I lit a cigarette and take a
drink of Johnny Walker. This was life.
Ex-wife's, ex-lovers, the innocent's of
what we were doing. There was no such
thing as destruction, only good times.

    Some people look at it as wasting
my life or my life's span, but I will
disagree with whomever at anytime. I
might have drank myself right now a
toast to bad health, but I lived a rich
life. I have seen where Hitler invaded
Europe, where the streets are paved

with water, America's major cities and
the filth that lived within. Now I sit
back in a place far from what I was
taught and still drinking, still living
life, well day to day.

A boring drive to somewhere, or nowhere?

I'm not sure where everything took a u turn on my life. I woke up one morning and could not move. I couldn't call into work let alone go. All I could think about was music and writing.

Two other guys and I had created a musical experiment that seemed to be catching on somewhat faster than anticipated. As a band and friends we were overjoyed, but not overwhelmed. The fellows and I were very optimistic about life and getting out of this city. This city is plagued in its fucking boredom and my heart explodes as I see it dying.

So we rehearsed and rehearsed, many times being shut down by the police, but always pushing the limits, the limits of this place. The band set a six month goal for us to reach. A six month goal to escape this city and all the trouble that we have created here, our demons.

The three of us needing out, needing to take that leap of faith that everybody was scared to take. So here we are, wondering what will happen next, what will we do next? Will people accept us, or are we going to end up on the wrong trail to success, to our passion. Whole heartedly believing in ourselves even as people doubt us we stay strong willed and ready. On this drive to where we are headed, we become more than a band, we start to become brothers. Fame, mansions, ten sport cars, none of this we crave, just a comfortable life that leads to living. Some freedom, but mainly living that odd choice that we decide to make as individuals. That action of faith. Could we do it? Is everybody right?

Either way it will be a long boring drive, that ends somewhere or nowhere just like everybody and their personal journey's, their quest. Maybe not. Maybe I have just created an imaginary path for myself to avoid reality, responsibilities. I'll wait and see where my next move takes me. I hope it's a long drive. I just hope it takes me to somewhere instead of nowhere.

Blacker than black

It's cold at night. I sit alone, smoking, drinking, and staring out at the dark. I sit by the window so I can see the smoke fill the air around me. I have become an old man.

I'm seventy two and have pissed it all away. I had it all, fame, fortune, good looks and nothing now. I sit in my big old house, the only thing I ever held on to when living in Europe and while traveling the world this house was it. Women use to call me all the time, unknown young beauties stopping by. These women had no idea who I was. Every once in awhile now a female fan would still look me up. I would disappoint them with my bitterness, my well known bitterness.

I was married once and I hated her. It was when I was thirty three and it was a mistake, then again I was to. I ruined the woman that I married, I ruined her life. I was smacked out when I married her and I was smacked out when she divorced me. Lisa, my ex, thought I was something I wasn't, I was her thought experiment. I believe Lisa loved me, but I think she loved what she heard of me. At one time she was charmed by my drinking, my readings and my mystery. My tattoos told stories at one time, now they were faded and old, the women aged with me.

Lisa found out what I was, a trapped lonely soul. I loved her look and the ways she fucked, but despised the fact that she couldn't see pass my exterior. Lisa found out that I had a black heart, it scared her, and it scared me. Lisa could tell when I was not telling the truth. "Where the fuck have you been? Why do you disappear for a few days's all the time? You are impossible to love.""That's because I hate me, you hate me, and the world despises me and my words."We divorced after six months. I wasn't upset. Lisa took almost half of my material, but not all my money.

I hid most of my royalties, deceiving her in more ways than she would ever know. Everything else I covered before she and I married. I paid her off to get the fuck out of my life and it was worth it. After the divorce I spent Almost a year hiding in

Paris. I spent my day's writing and drinking. I became ill at the age of forty. A rot gut and a," DRINKING PROBLEM," is what they told me, yet I'm Seventy two. The world has cursed me for many more years than I wanted.

Blowing through my money, fucking up my fame. I became impossible to work with and didn't want to be worked with. Money and fame can get to a man though, even worse when he has bad outlook on life anyway.

Now I'm seventy two and alone, doing what I do best. I look at the unopened letters that have stacked up by my desk. I still write for piss off money. I buy cheap booze and cheap cigarettes. I have no license, or dignity, just my writing, my opinions and imagination, but I'm not sure I even care anymore. I was taught different, so many forgotten years ago, but I still had a black, cold heart, I have grown one.

Carousel

I can still smell all the champagne in the air. The New Year hits and the Eiffel tower lights up and everybody pop's their cork and chants for the New Year.

I watch as lovers set the mood for the New Year. I sit down and drink my drink. I look over and see a beautiful carousel. The beauty was a symbolized figure of fun and innocents.

Everybody starts to head back to their hotels and homes. I stay behind like the stray that I am. The carousel stayed lit up along with tower and I just sat there. I don't know what I was thinking; I just remember the beauty, the happy thought of that moment.

After awhile the carousel light's shut off. The tower keeps glowing in the early morning hours. I feel sad for some reason, not because of loneliness, but for reason I didn't know yet and may never know. I get my flask of scotch out and head for the train in the cold darkness.

The train ride was quick and lost in my mind. I couldn't go home though, I couldn't go anywhere. All I could do was think about the carousel and the happiness it brought people. My face smiling as the kids riding it faces were smiling to and their family happiness. Maybe I found serenity in the thought of their smiles.

They start to clean the streets in the early morning hours, so I get up and go over to the carousel. It seemed so lifeless without the smiles, the night scene filled with bright lights. It was dead, at least for a few more hours. I was on a train though and all I had is the memory of the night of the carousel and it's loneliness as well as my sadness.

That Time

I miss that time that we didn't have to think so hard. Have we become the "Innocent Savages" that I had always feared we might. This seems to be a long walk for such a short path. I miss the time the walk made me smile and it couldn't have been long enough. The time that we had but never spent, like a dead currency. I miss the time that people paid me for, the never again hours of the day and the night. That time to get here and the questions that comes with it. I miss innocence, the time it was around and the role it played. It seems the world has become cruel, maybe my mind, only time will tell in a world like this. Trying to figure it all can help some, but others it is just more time lost, abandoned, stolen, killed, held hostage, or used for all the wrong reasons. I miss that time, a time I don't really know, and a time that may have been simpler. Hopefully I don't miss this time, but too much thinking about it does do it and then more passes.

Don't feel hurt for nothing

"Just give me the fucking knife. I promise everything will be alright. You don't need me". "Fuck you Mike; I'm tired of this shit, your shit. Go do what you want, go do who you want!" Her name was Heather. Heather and I had been messing around for the last couple of months. I was busy and hardly around, while Heather sat around waiting on me. She was always asking what I was doing.

Heather had it in her head that Heather and I were meant to be together. I naturally disagreed with her, not feeling the same way. Heather was beautiful, but her mind was long gone. She was always getting into some sort of drama. Maybe this is what attracted me to Heather to begin with? For whatever the reason be, Heather and I ended up here, in this situation.

"Heather just put the knife down and get out of the bathtub. I'm not worth dying over, nobody is worth dying for. Heather you are gorgeous, but you need help and I'm no fucking good for you." "Whatever Mike. You and your excuses can shut the fuck up." I was stuck. I didn't know how to handle this; she even threw my phone into the toilet. I guess that will teach me to leave the seat up. How did this start and end in my house? What will I do if she succeeds?

"Okay Heather, if you can't see the truth behind this drama then do what you have to. I'm tired. In fact I might do it after you, but it won't be a love story to write or hear about." I go into the kitchen and pour a tall one while smoking my cigarette and try to pull myself together. Heather had been fun, but we could not go on. She fell for me to hard to quick and I didn't. Heather always loved to hear me play guitar and read my writings, never questioning them. She seemed at first to be full of life. I decide that I am going to write her a poem about us, about life that we shared. If she won't listen to me, then maybe if I leave her a poem, then maybe she will realize that she doesn't have to feel hurt for nothing.

I know she hasn't committed the act yet and I hope I can get through to her before. Heather cries out and it hurts me to write the poem. I write a long poem, trying to symbolize love and all her good. I'm stuck though. I hear her cry out and I find myself not wanting to lie to her. If I lied to Heather just to get her out of the tub, then what would I do next? So I write from the heart, but that is a problem, but I let her know she is special and unique. I try to group the words together to make her understand that I am nothing. I am a bug on a car window in some wrecking yard. How do you tell someone this, how do you end this?

I finish writing the poem and finish my drink. I walk into the bathroom and Heather is still in the tub with my knife and she is sobbing, it hurts me. I tell her I love her in my way, but it was no good. "Heather, here is something that I wrote for you. I hope you will get out and read it." "Are you leaving Mike, where are you going?" "I don't know Heather. Probably somewhere where I can kill myself slowly, but I can't stay here and handle this if you won't let me. You know how I feel about you and me. Read the poem." Heather doesn't say anything and she stares at the wall, never looking at me.

I go to a bar down the road. A place that would not know me, a nowhere. I call my house and get no answer. I call it again, still no answer. I have another whiskey and smoke before trying again. I stumble to the phone and try once again. A man picks it up, a policeman. The policeman told me to come home. He said he needed to talk to me. I tell the man I will start to walk that way and then I ordered another tall one, sat down and tried not to think, but this was not an option. I get up and head for the door. A policeman opens the door. "Hello, I am Mike officer."

Day's

Sitting on my couch, with you and that's
alright,
I made a dollar, but spent two and that's
alright,
You never really knew that I despise you,
But that's okay, because I'm going to lie on
my couch for awhile, smoke my boredom gone
for awhile
But that's okay, because I'm alright
Just wasting another hello,
Seeing all of you from my way down below,
Hoping someday this mess will go away; most
importantly the thought of not thinking of
this is a great thought on its own.
The sky is blue, but needing it to be cloudy
To help me, help me feel that way,
The way you need to feel to write your true
thoughts.
The way a bottle of vodka releases those
demons that makes us all want to write or
say in the mirror.

Everyone's interest is stronger
Than mine

Away she goes, but I don't care
anymore. Diamond rings, new cars, houses,
marriage, these were not for me. My
interests are elsewhere. My interest lay in
a pit of the unknowing of tomorrow. I want
to yell wake up, wake up, but I have become
a mute. My mind, my words, everything.
American dreams just not what it seems to
me.

This ongoing battle of good and evil is
what makes me angry. What's wrong, what's
right? I try to leave out all my hate for I
am a mute. She goes, but I don't care
anymore.
I forget names, times, memories, but I
retain enough. Everybody talks to me and yet
I am still a mute, alone drowning in my
thoughts. Everybody's interest is stronger
than mine. I'm not sure if there is a name
for the place where my interest dwells. I
stress myself to my grave just like you, but
I'm hoping for the dead, or for you to wake
up. Away she went, but I don't care anymore,
my interest is not that strong.

I hope one day to have the pleasure of
being interested into something. Does it
exist in women, money, running away,
staying? I seem to waste the beautiful days
we are blessed to see and somehow I am okay
with this.

Vilify

Empty night on an empty head,
Too tired to go to bed,
What was I thinking?
Did I ever know?
We had the map, but never knew where to go
Never understood,
Never asked why,
Never really cared, just wasted time,
It was always a good time, smoked a
cigarette to ease my mind
Made that decision, just in time
But for now she forgot my name,
Probably forgot our night of shame,
Having no plan, no want to understand,
It all got old, needing to just let go,
But being gone this long can get to any man
I guess for now I'll fill this empty head
with booze and try to sleep
Another day away,
Another day that I have accomplished.
All of who are surprised, well fuck you,
fuck your congratulations.
Fuck your lower expectations you had of me
and still continue to have.
Family, friends, the will never read this,
only I can appreciate what I've done.
    Don't defame something that is nothing...

True

 I faintly remember those, "innocent," years of young love. It had a chapter in my life just like anyone else's. I write a lot of bitterness and drunken rages, but that's not my whole life. As I sit beside my bed and write this, I have a strange, strong memory. She was gorgeous and her name was Naomi. Naomi knew she was gorgeous and at other times she seemed to forget all her beauty. No matter what though, she always had to be the center of attention. As I sit and remember being 15 and Naomi was 17, I also think about the fact that I have whole other life now, as does she. I look at my bed and decide to write from there.

 It's like I want to feel some of those memories. The smell of the detergent from the sheets, being the same brand detergent that I use now still and bringing back so many memories. Mornings of her asking me to skip work and stay in bed with her and me getting fired once for that very scenario. I didn't care because she was warm, like the way you imagine home being.

 Naomi was always standing still and I on the other hand always had one foot out the door. Now the ironic thing was I was wishing I could get one foot in her door. I'm not a real sensitive man, nor am I a cold hearted man, but I sometimes wish for those days to come back. To lay on a lazy morning with her tiny body curled into my arms, my muse. To not worry about anything, because everything was lying in my arms.

Life has a cruel way of reminding me of the truth. The truth behind the reasons of why Naomi wasn't beside me in my bed. I do go many days without thinking of her, but then loneliness set's in as I think of her in someone else's arms. The unknown man who plays like an actor, as does Naomi. I sit on my bed writing and other thought's start to come, they don't over power those warm moments, but they come in to. Like the way she could be cold at times and hurtful in ways that seemed harsh at the time. Laying here though I can't or don't choose to care of those human, random acts that were inflicted. It's not a matter of what could have happened, because regretfully I believe I know what would have become of our love. These thoughts and wants are from good memories.

The reasons why you choose not to think of the bad times, when it was worth going through the pain for that faint scent in the air that reminds me of Naomi. Without the bad there would not have been any of the good. Life reminds me of the truth from time to time.

Forget about me

"It's always me," I yell as I walk out of Tiffany's apartment and down to the bar. I didn't want to argue with her anymore. It felt like life was too short to argue, yet we spend so much time doing just that. I didn't really know anymore about Tiffany, but she thought she really knew me.

A year ago I had too many materials, to many responsibilities. I was the one who placed me into that awful spot. I worked hard for everything I had, but I was not happy. "Nice house and car Mike, how is your shop doing?" Materials become these obsessions and then we have to exceed these limits. Tonight though, I knew I would be cold and lonely, walking the streets, having nowhere to go, nobody to go to. After Tiffany, I gave it all up. Every bit. I sold everything and wanted to be nobody, or continue to. So I head for Europe, with a dream in my head and a whole in my heart. I had dreams of creating something wonderful.

Now I find myself walking the streets of Amsterdam. A Dutch woman had been housing me for the past four months. It ended the same way it did with Tiffany and everyone before this. The chaotic voice of life always called my name. Who knows where I'll be tomorrow? I feel like I'm knocking on the wrong doors. I can't make a woman like Tiffany love me and I can't or maybe don't want that with a Dutch whore. I think about Tiffany everyday as she has married and longed moved on. I know I would have never forgived myself if I didn't try and accomplish my dreams and fears. Did I rob myself of something though? Did I waste too much time here or there? I don't mind being a penniless writer in a small flat, but I still think of her. Her smile and the way she curled in my arms.

I guess I'll see where I am tomorrow

Hidden message

"Mike I want to love you but you hate yourself so much that it is impossible to attempt to even try." She was right I did hate myself. I'm sorry and wish she could forgive me and leave me if she could. We had some good times, but only when we were fucking. I wish she would believe me if she could. She didn't know that I had grown to love our fucked up relationship.

Insecurity will drive a woman mad. A man cannot live when his every move is monitored and you only get one turn. I wish she didn't care what I did and didn't do. I write about her though. She doesn't know I don't even know if she has ever even read any of my writings, my soul. She had me in the palm of her hand, but she didn't know this. "Mike I wish you would talk to me let me in." "I don't know how to talk." "You can sure as fuck write,

but you're quite and alone." I always
had a hidden message when I wrote about
her and there was always a hidden
message about a boy who loved a girl.
If she would only read, but I fear
reading is no longer important to the
masses. The idiot box can tell you
right away what you want to hear and
what, "they," want you to know. The
beauty of reading is the independent
thought, the passion, the hate, the
muse that inspired so many. Inspired
people so much that they wrote about
their life, the up's and down's. There
are many hidden messages, but writers
also wear their heart on their sleeves
leaving their selves open.

        I could never tell her or anybody
else what I think of them, but somehow
it's okay for them to tell me what they
think of me. This somehow sets fine
with me.

House on the hill

I sit and listen to the traffic in the early morning hours. People going to their jobs. On summer evenings I can hear people out on the lake a couple blocks behind me. Most of the year you can hear the ice cream man rolling around. I sit; sit looking out my windows at my writing desk. The double windows are on the second floor of the house on the hill, so they oversee the neighbors, while hiding me. My entire yard is fenced off, like I have something to hide. Only my privacy

My dog lies at the top of the drive way and barks at anybody walking by. I sit out in my garage, or on the deck drinking countless hours away. I've fought twice in my front lawn with friends, some bare knuckle boxing. When I'm not working, I spend most of my time at my house on the hill. It's become my haven. I write, read, fuck, play music, record, drink and sleep there. Past two stop signs and then on your left it's the house on the hill

Ash on the end
Of her
Cigarette

It was a typical Saturday morning, I
was hung-over of course. I had been in a bit
of a rut lately, keeping myself in
isolation, I was in need of an outing. My
friend Haus calls me and says he is having a
party. I normally wouldn't go to a party
like this, one that was infested with close
minded suburbanites. I venture out though
and show up around 11 pm, a little buzzed
and actually happy to see some old faces.
I see an old buddy who I've actually been in
trouble with down in Mexico and he wants to
head over towards his truck. I had figured
he had a joint or blunt to smoke. I sit down
in the passenger side and my friend gets in
the driver's side and turns on the radio.

"You want to do some coke?" my friend
had asked me. I told him those days were far
behind me. "Come on, just a little for old
times' sake." I told him that I couldn't
handle myself anymore on that shit. He
backed off and did the four rails he had
laid out. I am smoking like crazy, for one I
didn't like any of the people there and two
this wasn't the kind of mindless chatter I
choose to engage in. I smoke a joint as my
old friend snorts up his paycheck and then
he proceeds to talk about the old days.

About all the shit that I had pushed far away from my mind, all these memories I had disconnected me from.

I was still on pins and needles when right on cue, they pulled up the cops. Luckily we were parked on the end of the line of cars, in fact they showed up because some of the cars were parked, facing the wrong direction.

The road beside the house with all the cars, the road didn't even have a center stripe, so the cops were just being dicks. My old friend is freaking out, but suddenly jumps out of the truck. I light a cigarette and walked over away from the crowd by the fuzz. I look and my old friend was chattering away with the police as fast as he could spit it out and he actually pulled it together and pulled it off. I on the other hand was just sitting back. I was over twenty one; in fact nobody was under twenty one, for the reason at hand. Finally the police start to leave after telling us not to drive and they would be checking on us by posting guard. About that time some stupid frat boy takes a piss on the front side of the car and of course had the police all worked up. He got what his dumbass deserved, basically an expensive piss, then the police left.

The lack of good conversation and good booze had me bored. I start to leave and I hear, "Mike, Mike, is that you?" I see the girl and it takes a few minutes for me to get through the fog in my mind. I look hard and remember her face and start to remember our chapter in life previously before. It comes to me in bits and pieces, but her name doesn't come to me. She had no grudge against me; in fact she was excited and even frisky with me. I feel bad because I can't even call her by her name. The girl was sexy and pretty, but in a different way, a certain sassy attitude that I started remembering. We decide to seek refuge in the darkness of the backyard and smoke a joint together. The whole time she is surprised to see me, excited to see me, for what reason I did not know, but I liked it. Then she tells me about the last time we saw each other. The last time was during the early morning hours two years previously, at the end of January. It starts coming back to me.

Two years before this I was good friends with this woman, kind of a friend with benefits. On the morning before I left for Paris, we had connected like never before and I remember I was sad because in a way I knew it was over for a while or maybe for good.

I left after she fell asleep, sliding out the door. That brings us to two years later with a beautiful girl and no name in my selfish soul to mutter. She leans in and kisses my neck and proceeds to let me know I'm welcome to come on in. After a bit we are sitting together, not really talking and she asked if she could have one of my cigarettes, so she didn't have to go into the house for hers. We looked up at the polluted sky, feeling nice and had learned from her that she and I were very much alike. She was a couple of years older and I felt we were both more mature, but she had a boyfriend and even though she liked me, I am what I am. I am a little depressed, when I look up at her pretty face in the moonlight smoking a cigarette, every move seemed to be sexier than regular movement should be. Some ash falls from the cigarette onto my lap and I remember her name. Ashley, my little blond lover, who was so good to me and I was so bad to her.

I needed that night, but I have a feeling Ashley didn't. Maybe she saw the loneliness in my eyes, or maybe she just wanted to fuck. Either way she always seems to cross my path when I need her to. As I ash the cigarette while writing in the early morning hours, I wish our paths would cross again soon, real soon.

I like to hear a little guitar

The sweet smell of rain comes through my window during these early morning hours. Most mornings I get up and do my routine, but this morning I just wanted silence. I made a pot of coffee and roll up a blunt. I drank some coffee while I smoked my blunt and listened to the beautiful sound of the light rain. Weather like this always made me smile, it fit my personality. It's like the rain was soft descent music to my ears.

As the high kicks in I begin feeling a kind of serenity in the calmness. I smoke a couple of cigarettes and finish my coffee. The rain went from a light rain to a heavy rain. The rain started to seem like a tribal beat. I went inside from my balcony and grab my guitar and my harmonica. I planted my ass on the balcony and start to play whatever came to my simple mind. I didn't want to hear my weak voice, so I just played

with the rain, my guitar sounded great;
it was nice like the rain was singing
for me.

It was a great morning. I didn't
even call into work as I sat there and
listened to the sweet sound of my
guitar and knew that if I didn't answer
the phone that life would be okay.
Maybe I could sit there and dream about
making a living at playing some guitar.
I would bet green money that people
will never get my music and to them I
ask where is there musical talent. Some
musicians surpass me but they lack the
soul that I have, the love. You can try
to break my heart for my music but
never fucking lie to me. You killed my
descent music that was playing as I
die.

I'll play a little guitar for you
and you play a little guitar for me and
maybe one day somebody with endless
soul with appreciate the self respect
as a true artist

Starlight

I lay on the ground looking up at the
stars. I look and I remember all the times
I've laid watching the stars. The times out
of depression, but mostly the young love
that I've shared those moments looking at
the stars with. It makes me smile as I think
back. I start to remember the faces I have
forgotten over what has now become years.

Laying on the ground, trampolines,
rooftops, whatever we could do to get out of
site to experiment. There was something
about the time, the age, and the innocents
of curiosity, it made life fun. No stress
really, just the thought of some girl who
would break your heart and then the next
after that. It was fun for many reasons, but
the mystery of the human chemistry was what
made those cruel, but still fun years. An
example for instance was being in a pool at
night alone with a girl. We were always hid
by the starlight and water, rubbing our wet
bodies together for the first time.

Then we grow and the simplicity of this
once comforting act becomes a distant
memory. Life becomes complicating, losing
any wonders that we had. The world can keep
going where it's going and I can go mine.
One thing I'll always have is my starlight
memories and the thought of more.

I look forward to finding that girl
worthy of spending simple moments with. At
twenty eight years old I put my faith in
believing that this moment can still be

achieved. Not with a groupie or common
barfly, but a lost soul looking for another
true lost soul. Starlight will light my
night up again one day.

I need her moment

She's seductive; she teases me
constantly and never listens. I love
the way she fucks, the way she taste.
I haven't seen her in months though, or
even heard from her.

   "You're the only one who truly
understands my soul. I wish we were
together, at least for the moment." It
doesn't bother me when she says that, I
would take advantage even for her
moment. She knows who she is. I've
wrote countless stories of her and she
always knows when I write of our
chapter in life. She flatters me when
she tells me she loves my stories, that
she loves me. I loved her as well. "I
need to see you, I miss our time."
"You know all you have to do is call me
and we can have that moment," I tell
her. The thought of her taste and smell
arouses me.

   The call never comes; she chooses
to disappoint me every time. We know
were not made for each other, but we
know we had a rare connection. I wish

her so much luck, but all I can think about is the last time a couple years ago when she gave herself to me and I took her. I took her for as long as she would have me on that night.

I light a cigarette as I walk towards my car. She was smoking in her doorway as she waved one last good bye. I wish I could see her in her doorway, smiling, smoking, with her hair hanging over one side of her face, seductive, I prayed for one more time at least. It's hard though. I know she wants me and I know I want her. I'm afraid of certain things though as the years pass. I'm afraid we'll never share that moment again, that silence as we smoke and listen to music, lying as one.

For now I'll have to wait for her call, for that moment I hope she calls me for. She could choose to never have that moment with me and instead bless somebody else with it, but I'm the one who truly understands her soul. She is the only one who thinks she knows me and I love her for her trying to comprehend my simple yet complex mind.

I thought you would want it

"Mike what were you thinking, was it the drinking, being alone? Come on man get your head together". This was all I could sit there and tell myself; unfortunately it was not the first time. She was beautiful and I was nothing and I had nothing. No laughter, joy, passion, friendship, just me. It was a cold slap to the face.

Brown Eyes

    I look at her, stare at her.
Sometimes I look at her all day. She
never makes me mad; sometimes we had
become depressed together about the
things going on around us. There has
never been an obsession so deep in my
heart. I remember when I first looked
at her, the first time I held her. It
seemed weird at first, but then grew on
me quickly. She was exciting; she made
my life fun again. I wondered how many
other people she made feel this way,
maybe I was the only one, that one
special one.

    I began to love her and became
upset when I had to leave her side. She
makes me want to play with her all day.
I call her Brown Eye's and do this for
many glorious years. She brought much
happiness to me, but there are problems
that come with happiness. There are too
many reasons why she couldn't stop
this. Like most people, especially

women in my life, I push them away. I
push them away with my drinking, my
selfishness, sometimes my passions.
I'm sorry my Brown Eye's, I loved you,
I still love you. I didn't mean to get
drunk and slam you against the floor.
Sometimes the music will make a man
ruin a perfectly good guitar.

I'm lonely for the big town

"Mike I'm bored, take me out, I've been cooped up here for days". "I leave for Europe in two days Linda; I'm fine where I'm at. I don't want any fucking shit coming from you before I go. Go out your fucking self". Linda had been around too long and was becoming a problem. I was lonely for the big town, for the loneliness of the big town. I live in the city, but I needed a new one, one where I'm not known, or noticed. Linda was just trying to mind fuck me before leaving for Amsterdam. Getting me mad is an easy way for her to be at peace with her actions when I'm gone. The act of something that no man wanted to hear.

It's not so much the women who get to me, it's me. I can't help that they always choose to hate me, but that's not really my problem. I don't owe her or anybody anything. I need that big town. I need to not be thought about. I had my life to get together, to figure out what I was supposed to do. Instead

I had set back for too long listening
to other's and there little problems.
No complex questions about life, just
shit they wanted to bitch about. I need
that big town. These people have easy
answers; maybe that's why I have
avoided my own problems. Maybe that's
why I have too many people coming to
me, getting mad at me?

Linda didn't need me and I didn't
need Linda. It was just a short story
with no point to it. It's not sad it's
life, truth; it's for the sake of
passion, not for drama and heartache.
I'm lonely for the big town. I'm tired
of the carbon copy people I see every
day. Today would be a good day to pack
more than just my suitcase. I think
today would be a good day to start
packing everything for the big town.

Sunsets are goodbyes

I'm starring out the back window,
on a cold winter evening. I'm starring
at the sunset as I pop a couple of
pills and pour a drink. I pour a tall
one and lit a big one. At this moment,
the sunset depresses me and also brings
relief to my soul.

I start to realize that ever
sunset is really a goodbye. It is the
last hours that day have to offer, no
more after that. It's a chance to
forget about your problems for one more
night. For some people it is their last
night. Their last night on earth,
whether it's suicide, fate, or an
accident. This part disturbs me. I take
too much; do too much to press the
outer limits. For all the rest, they
look at sunsets and feel like they have
accomplished life for one more day. So
they look at it, relax and enjoy. For
the rest of us, sunsets are goodbyes

For the rest sunsets could be
hello for the next day that hopefully

follows. There are two types of people in this world, people who can sit and enjoy the sunset and people who cannot.

Contradictions

Fast to talk, slow to move, saying the
things you won't do, protesting the
things you can't prove.

Center of attention is where you want
to be, opinions and bullshit that don't
appeal to me.

What would you do if you were put on
the spot? Could you pull it off, or is
it once again talk?

War, peace, you'll never know, you poor
bastard you just do what you are told
and miss-phrase when you repeated

Instant Animosity

Driving in rush hour traffic, I'm alright, smoking a joint listening to Baboon, just sitting it out. I look at the people in their cars around me and they seem to all be in a hurry. To where? Maybe I'm jealous because I have nowhere to be. I let people around; I even let myself get pushed back in the dreadful line that seems endless. Most are business men leaving downtown, or mad mothers in minivans.

Maybe the weed helps settle me down from this chaos, the others might be hurrying to theirs? I see a sign that says right lane closed two miles ahead. Every car is shooting through that right lane to get ahead. This causes, what I like to call, A STUPID FUCKING TRAFFIC JAM. I let some in and piss the others off. Most of the cars that are flying through there are in wrecked cars. I laugh, turn the radio off and laugh. The stupid people can't help it. Their stupidity spreads like cancer.

It starts to get ridiculous, the sun is setting and the beer, somewhere, is cold. I had enough off the passing right lane, for these people to cause this unnecessary jam, so I pull out in between my lane and the shoulder. People slam on their brakes and you can smell burnt rubber tires in the air. I get fingers flying up from everybody behind me and I smile, waving, wondering why they are so mad. So quick to hate. My mother use to whip the shit out of me just for saying hate. I laugh and finish my joint, letting the music take over as I pass the time.

I remember a man who had been beaten and left dead during a road rage incident. This poor man, with a family was run off the road and beaten to death. This is Texas for fuck sake, they will fry a bastard, but the roads use to be friendly. Hell I heard once that the French even liked Texans until a well known Texan fucked that up for eight years. The French have always been kind, but like anybody else, nobody wants you on their turf, but will take your money if given the chance. Remembering this and other vicious, needless crimes, along with the mob of commuters behind me, I started to see what had become a permanent trait of the human mind. It was animosity. The power to instantly have so much animosity. Not energy, not faith, not passion, just pure lack of the respect of mankind.

Just stay away

What makes an obsession healthy, or unhealthy? There was this girl named Ashley, who had been a thorn in my side. She had captivated me and then ignored me. Not in a bad way, just ignored. I didn't like to think about her. Ash has a boyfriend and I figure it was best to stay away from our friendship. Our friendship had become nothing to her, but I tried sometimes. I was jealous, because I had never had a woman love me the way she seem to love her boyfriend. I had to respect that. Ash had invited me a couple of times, downtown, to meet her boyfriend and have a beer. I couldn't do it. See her sitting there with another person. We weren't meant to be together, I am too selfish, but you want what you want.

Life had been doing its normal routine on me, so I decided to go pick my buddy up. We went downtown, to a bar that was over crowded, but we just observed and made fun of people. We talked some, but not much, that's why we were friends. I went to the bathroom after having a few beers and make my way up the stairs. There sitting on my chair was Ash. She was smoking a cigarette and drinking. She hugged me, me being hesitant. Her hair and neck smelt so good, just like when we use to lay naked getting high laughing at stupid things. We talk for a moment and then she has to go back down stairs to her boyfriend. I'm glad though. All I would have done is hurt one of us. I lit a cigarette and finished my beer. I want to leave, so we head for the door. I duck my head not wanting to see them; instead I just wanted to go home, but that was not what the fate of this night had in store for me.

No this night landed me in jail. I don't know if it was me not being able to see Ash and handle it sober, or if it was an arrest like all the rest, out of stupidity. I spent a few days in jail, lost in the system, what Tarrant county was known for. I couldn't ever see her again, knowing I would probably end up in some sort of isolation. It happened to often.

To the man who
Lived at the
Bottom of a bottle

I knew a man named Harold, who seemed to be just there. I seen him a lot, but he is always drunk. You can tell that life was not always so harsh on him, I imagine life kicked the piss out of him a time or two. It seemed as if he forgot the real world from his earth. I set back and wonder his background, his life history and why he looks freshly beat by life. Maybe a divorce or a death, but he almost looks like he has a story to tell from the bottom of his bottle.

I decide to ask him one afternoon what he use to do for a living. Harold told me he had done many things, but he mostly was hired as a bouncer for whores. I begin to hear the awful, but interesting stories that this man mutters out. He does not care and probably wants me to leave him alone, but I don't care. He tells me of a Mexican whore, that about three years ago he was her bodyguard, down in boy's town.

He proceeds to tell me about a few young guys who went down there to party and that he got the scar on his face from that and also got his elbow broken during the same confrontation. Harold said it started because the guy didn't follow the time limit and then the guys kept getting the girls coked out.

Harold told me that if he ever seen any of those guys again, that he was going to kill them and he looked like he could if given

the chance. I get a bottle and raise my
glass for a toast, to fry those bastards
when he catches them.

I leave him at the bottom of my bottle
and I get up and leave the small bar in
Southwest Texas and head out on the road to
get a cheap motel. I was feeling good and
was glad that I had met Harold. It reminds
me of the life that I don't want to get
into. Life is already a bitch. But I would
have been one of the assholes young guy's
had I chose that life.

                    Never fell asleep
                      With the
                       T.V. on

          Out of money and out of time
Out of this town, out of this mind
That's okay, we weren't having fun anyway
Remember leaving? It was forever
You're always thinking the thought, just
none of them being me,
You kept me awake at night with your T.V.
Never considering what you were doing to me
Wanting to join you and millions with your
heads in the clouds,
But you never knew what you were doing to me
with your T.V.,
Everything will fall into place, maybe it
will just float into place,
I daydream of that night when you and many
others don't depend on such an evil device.
I ask myself though if my writing is an evil
device.
There are many reasons why I don't have to
worry about that.
The main one being, nobody reads my
writings, my gibberish.

Deluge of Dilettantes

       Well I didn't know, I didn't want to
say,
About what happened in the world today?
Just another person that's been converted to
you, always changing, you were never true,
but now that I'm here I see it so clear,
there was no art, was no passion, just you
and your fucked up fashion.
       .....dilettante's was all that I could
see, the same clueless faces starring back
at me, we thought we were different, but we
are all the fucking same.
Guessing we will have to wait out the days,
wait out the ways. Could this be changed, or
what has taken place so far, will it forever
take place now.

Who are you??

Cat like thief

   She is no longer worth writing
about; she is no longer worthy of
having a name, or a spot in my mind to
want to write about, to remember. She
said she was done with me in a letter.
I started to apologize, but I didn't
know why. She made me fall in love with
her, but she could never love me, I
could never love me.

   Now the world is hers to go back
to fucking. No more poems wrote while
driving, listening to her voice inside
my head. I miss her, but grow bitter as
I hear she fucked someone else. I call
a whore or two to ease the pain, but I
am cursed in this place, this plague.
"You don't want to be with me, you show
me that every day." She picks fights,
wanting me to say what she wants to,
but she is scared to let me go until
one day she explodes or finds better.

   She killed me in her letter,
ripping my heart out from behind. This
is the finally, the big end for me,
nothing for her to care about. I will

learn to hate her some day, I hope, but until then these little white pills help.

This is my, or should I say our suicide note pertaining to our relationship. She killed us. She didn't do it with grace; she did it like a thief in the night, never giving me the chance. So as I get closer to dying alone, I curse her. The poems never made her smile anyway. She always turned beautiful writings of love into hatred.

She is nobody, I am nobody...

Nobody cares

"SO SHUT THE FUCK UP"

Pretend its all okay

Another morning waking up feeling like somebody has beaten the shit out of me. I spend my mornings over the toilet puking blood. After I get past the rot gut, I go for a beer to help settle my stomach. "Mike you need to stop drinking. With your stomach you could cause some serious damage to your body." There is no drug that can help me escape the harsh reality of this cruel confusing world. The choice was mine I didn't think enough, but I'm too depressed to go on. I try to pretend, but I can't wait to get outside this world. I just want to pass the time alone. I write this knowing nobody will read it, or even care how I survive past this alone, the way I like for things to be.

I use to have goals, missions, but time went away. Where does time go? I make excuses, but in the end it's fucking useless, an empty thought. I'm

sorry, but who am I sorry to? Who
remembers me? If I die tonight, who
will care, would I be forgotten in a
month. My shades are pulled shut
though; my words are just rotting and
falling away. I never fix the problem,
I never solve them. Maybe I gave it all
away one night when I was fucked up.
The nameless women just want me as a
novelty, a short boring chapter of
their lives. It's not right, but I play
the role. Sometimes I do miss me. I
find serenity in the darkness of my six
strings, the darkness of writing,
wondering where you went. Will somebody
come back and waste their time on me.
When I'm by myself I'm alone, when
people are around I'm alone. Sometimes
I wish I could find someone to breathe
in as I breathe out.

I had a girlfriend once that had
begged me to go to the doctor. She was
a great, caring woman. "If I don't get
better in a month I will go baby." "No
you won't Mike! This has already gone
on for too long as it is. I guess I
have no say in it though." I lied to
her and never went. I'll pretend and
keep her from wasting her time on me.

Too much reminds me of her

I pass by a woman at the bar who smells like Naomi always smelt, or wore the same perfume; it just didn't smell as good as it did on Naomi. I can't get her out of my mind. I need to leave, but I can't go home. The only way I can go home is to throw half of my possessions away. There is too much there to look at. The pictures, dead plants, dead air, dead passion.

I can't handle the thought anymore. The thought of her getting fucked by another man. The thought of her looking at another man the way she use to look at me. It was torture either way. There was no freedom. If we stayed together, then we would fight, but I could not stand the thought of her anymore, it surprises me. I could not run from my mind, but I could get away from everything that reminded me of her.

I pull into my driveway, remembering all the times we had, all

the places that we had fucked in my
house. I go in and get a beer and sit
down. I grab my stash and roll up a
blunt. I couldn't even watch the idiot
box to escape; I'm not an idiot I
guess, at least not in that way. Too
much reminded of her. I smoke some of
the blunt and drink a couple of beers.
I let my dog out the front door and I
throw the rest of the blunt on the
couch. The couch started to fill the
room with smoke, and then a flame
started to grow on it. I grab another
beer as the flame starts to take over
the living room. My memories start to
rest, my body loosens. I grab my last
beer and toast it to the past. The
upstairs start to catch the contagious
cleansing flame, always cleansing. I go
through the backdoor and grab a clean
shirt on my way out. I met my dog in
the front lawn. I drank the beer and we
both watched as a whole other life went
into flames. I had to get ready for the
fire department and the police, but I
wanted to enjoy the sight for just a
minute. The sight of that new life.

I no longer had to ask myself if I
wanted to throw something sentimental
away forever, because it was being
done. I was ready to start a new life,

a bed I haven't fucked her in and most
important is the distance that is now
being forced on us, I can only hope.
No longer would I see her as much. I'm
gone when the smoke clears...........

You ever go nowhere?

I was in the mountains, cold but not alone. "Mike you okay?" I was cold I needed to warm up. All I have on is jeans, no shirt or shoes. I look up and see the fuzzy face and I think it is my friend Brandon. We seem to go somewhere and the heat starts to become unbearable.

"Mike what are you doing?" "I don't know, what do you mean?" By this time I see about five fuzzy faces and one comes at me. I defend myself but can't seem to hit him and it was so hot. Then I see a familiar face. Heather, was she sent to get me out? "Mike what are you doing? You're late and why did you never show up?" "Where am I suppose to be and why is it so hot?" Heather disappears into darkness.

I start to feel a hot darkness closing in on me. It keeps closing in on me, frightening me. I was confused and lost. Had somebody drugged me and taken me somewhere, maybe nowhere?

Another fuzzy face tells me something
just as fuzzy as his face as he speaks
confusing me even more. I walk seeing
the highway. The highway looks thin and
dangerous, but I have to cross it, I'm
not sure why.

   The street begins to fall apart
yet somehow I made it across, still
feeling so hot. I see a friend not sure
who it is I began to run towards them.
I keep running but cannot reach this
person.

   Suddenly I wake up in my bed with
my sheets stuck to me by the sweat
dripping off of my body. I take a drink
off of the bottle of vodka lying beside
my bed. Nobody had drugged me. I'm a
nobody; it was cold all of a sudden.

Paris, she hardly knew you

Leaving Paris once again on a train headed to Amsterdam. Paris is great, but I prefer Amsterdam. It fits me better. I had taken a break from writing, drinking and my headphones. She was Dutch. As soon as I took my headphones off, I could hear her on her cell phone. Even though she was Dutch, she was speaking in English. Apparently this woman had gone to Paris with four other girls to celebrate the New Year.

The woman was upset though. She wanted to be at home with her other friends. She said the only way she would want to go back, is if she went with a man. I put my headphones back on and look out at the scenery arrangements changing. I think of all the times in Paris. The cobblestone, the history, the great wine and I didn't understand how she could have not liked Paris. The first time and every time it's captivating no matter what. There was something fascinating everywhere you looked. I feel sorry for

that girl not exploring Paris, all the
way down to the underground world.
Maybe that underworld of Paris was what
she was looking for, or needed? Some
people get bored easy and maybe she
just didn't like the streets of Paris.
At least what you see.

Shut your sinner mouth

I tell her everything that she wants to hear. I let her talk as much as she wants to. I agree with everything, making everything seem more than it is. I just want to be another lover, so I listen. When she asked me about myself, I tell her what she wants to hear. She becomes intrigued and it sparks the fire. It's always fun, but turns quickly. I had no idea who was telling the truth and who was full of shit. I finally came to the conclusion that she and I thought we were playing each other. We were though. She knew how to get under my skin. I knew she never acted on her threats, no that would chase me away forever. I never had a woman treat me that way ever.

The cruelness always came out of her though. "Fuck You Mike, this is the last time." She would stick her middle finger right in front of my face. She would tell me to get out of the car to many miles each time from my house. Somehow she always wanted to forget about the mess that she has created. Claiming to love me, but admitted to hating me to….

If I listen real hard

I admit that I don't really have a clue. "You never listen to me Mike, you're selfish." This was true. I failed to hear other people. I believe it to be the lack of interest, but others never understand that and why should they? "No, I'm supposed to care when you come over with your opinions and I don't want to hear them. Look Heather I don't know what to say at this point."

I told her when I met her that I grow tired of people and she was a person. Heather did not like this statement; I could see it in her eyes right away. "One of these days Mike you will have to join the rest of the world, it's not just about you." "Well babe it isn't about you either, so FUCK OFF." Heather leaves like all the rest. I think a part of me hurt's when they left me. I always got tired of them, I push them away and then I want them back. As I take a drink, I realize that it's the worst feeling, loneliness. Yet some women made me want to be alone.

I remember in high school once that I had a thing for a hot piece of ass. I listened to her at first to fuck her. She was a great fuck. I figure it was because she was to experienced for a girl her age. We would meet up and fuck, but I fucked it up by taking her out once. I listened to her actually talk. She was a selfish person and mean. I took her home while she sucked my dick. We pulled into her parents parking lot and she started to get out. "I'm glad we fucked, but you have a terrible heart. Listen to yourself some time."

The song I never wrote about her

Lindsay was great. It almost worried me how similar we are. I love talking to her; something about her made you not want her to stop talking. This is a rarity in this day and age that I live in. Conversation is a dying art.

Nobody's reads anymore, in fact I'm surprised that you are reading this right now. Not to call my generation stupid, maybe misguided, but still a unique generation we are. Lindsay, she read everything I wrote and other author's as well that we both liked and respected. She was very well read and insightful. Lindsay was out living life like me, taking every opportunity that life would throw at me, never wanting to never question what would have happened.

I probably don't have to say this, but Lindsay was not mine, my girl that

is. No she was captivated with a lucky
fucker. The bastard has probably never
heard of Bukowski. I believed I loved
her and started believing that she
would fall for me. Her boyfriend never
had the pleasure of having the deep
conversations that I had with her, at
least I hope not. That was her guy's
loss though.

I started running into Lindsay
more and more when she moved back to
the city. She would come over and watch
the band rehearse, and she was always
there. After hanging out with Lindsay I
would drink and play my acoustic
guitar, hidden in the dark from
everybody still hanging around
drinking. I would think about her and
look at a picture I had of us that was
taken after a gig. It was there with
other pictures, but hers would stick
out the most. I would play beautiful
sounding chords and just play,
sometimes singing, just thinking of
her, but inspiration is odd. It was
hard to have a muse that could never be
mine and seemed weird to write about
nothing. That's a hard thought to
except. Who knows why I would play and
think of her and never had anything

come out of it? It's hard to write
about nothing.

　　I never wrote down the lyrics that
I sang about her. No every time I sang
about her it was the same, never having
to be reminded of how special she is. I
wonder what I would call the song?

Anger is a gift

I have a neighbor named Ken and he is always happy. He talks and talks at the fence line with me and his old war encounters. He's in his sixty's, gray hair, badly trimmed mustache, and of course a perfect lawn. "Mike how are you doing today?" "I had a long, but great day myself". I'm not good at small talk, but I try, at least try and feel I am a good neighbor for all the shit I cause. Ken never has a beer and doesn't smoke, just seems high on life. My question is when does he let anger go? I believe that everybody gets angry, upset, a bad day, something. Maybe some people figure out their key to their happiness. That is a pleasant, but hard thought.

My other neighbor, Dave, Is happy, or mad half the time. He comes out yelling at time at his dogs. Other times we meet on the other fence line for a beer. Dave is happy drinking a beer working in his shop and you can tell he likes the work, even when he complains. Both neighbors had to take some time to like me. I moved in and the band rehearsed there. I've had the cops over for me kicking the lead singers' ass.

Sometimes I get angry and it starts to scare me. Sure I can sit back and enjoy life at times to, but I get annoyed at other people. The way they drive like the road was built for them alone. The people who cut in lines, rubberneckers, authority. I don't watch TV anymore because of the senseless angry it brought me. The Hollywood celebrities and their pointless lives, every one of them liars. They want to talk about going green for mother earth, yet they use more natural resources and deplete so much that could be used for the causes they speak for.

I'm not an angry man. I don't walk around hating anything that I can find a flaw in. Anger is a gift. Without people like me getting angry over these fake, rich, spoiled people, nothing would really get resolved. The masses have turned into one ball of Liars and dilettantes. They do as their told, never asking why, never caring. Caring is not listening to a celebrity and shaking your head up and down, they just put their opinions in your head. Once again anger is a gift. When it calls for anger, it calls for truth.

I am a cross breed between Ken and Dave. I love life. I can't truthfully smile all the time. On the other hand, I can't walk around with a chip on my shoulder. That's when they form a mutiny. No I get angry when mankind has no regards for others. I hope that day comes when anger is a gift, not a tool for chaos and destruction.

A year went by and I never even tried

Jana was somewhat of a kind, gentle person, but also a true person. She had her mysterious yet obvious ways. I grew to love her some in some of those ways, probably her mysterious side, sometimes not knowing is better to me. All the same she grew on me, a visible disease. Jana would torture my sensitive soul, my little unknown spot that I regrettable showed her once. I'm only human and was alone, too alone.

I met Jana a year ago today and she ended whatever it was that we had today a year ago. Jana was a woman in distress and I heard the distress call when I met her. She interested me at first and almost captivated me. There were just a few problems, one being the fact she was still sleeping with her ex and I'm not a double dipper. I need

time for her to start becoming pure
again before a woman meets me. Jana
fucked him though and I fucked whoever
and we would meet up and drink. We were
each other's back burners; late night
calls for one reason only, no real
passion of truth to this action.

A few months past in routine,
perfect for me to do my thing and still
have a companion on call. I would
listen when Jana would cry about her
boyfriend, I wouldn't judge, I was just
being a friend. There is only so much a
man can take when hearing about other
people's problems; sometimes people
need to work stuff out on their own.
As Jana was finally let go by her
boyfriend, she came to me, she came to
me every day. Jana was insecure; she
needed somebody, somebody she can call
at anytime.

I feel like I'm a good person, but
not the right one for any woman. She
wasted her time on me though, choosing
to play with my emotions. After Naomi
moved away I said I would never take
that type of drama, hurt, or anger
again. Jana was different though, not
in being an individual, but different,
a female drinking buddy. Jana claimed
to love me, to want me and me only, but

I couldn't do that, so she chooses to seek comfort from her ex once again, like so many times before. It bothered me, but she told me once that all I had to do was change. I can't change something that I don't know, but I was told it was that easy.

I began to love Jana after eight months of the same routine. Jana became bitter and jealous for no reason, just insecurity. "Are you sleeping with someone?" "No." "Okay smart ass, then is someone sleeping with you? Your roommate wakes up to unknown girls from your shows and you didn't want me to come, but you let heather."

This started occurring every day, every day I was threatened. Jana began to try and torchure me with jealousy, but I kept my poker face on and played the hard ass. This lasted up until thirty minutes ago. I can't handle this abuse on my sanity anymore. Everything was fucked up and nothing was alright, I had to walk alone. "Please never talk to me again. It's sad you pushed me away with silence. You never even tried to treat me like a girlfriend, so stay the fuck away. I know you think I'm a sheep, but I have friends and you are the asshole that's what you warned me

you were. This letter is it; I don't
want you to write me and try to make me
feel bad anymore. We lied to each other
to much." I was surprised she was half
ass truthful. I treated her good
though.

I'm starting to open my friend
Johnny Walker to float through the busy
afternoon. I had to be in the studio to
do tracks in an hour and a half and I
felt like shit. I sit here smoking,
drinking, unfocused on the day's
agenda. So I sit down real quick and
began to write, listening to music
shutting out the depression that would
slip in if I let it in.

It's been six hours now since I
received the email. I drank out of my
flask as I head downtown. The rest of
the band had been drinking beer, but I
was fucked up on scotch and knew I was.
I somehow pull it off as we lay down
some tracks, keeping my
professionalism. I spend a few hours
with the band and head back. I opened
my laptop and see this story sitting
there on the screen and I read it. I
read her email I printed out and seen
through my drunken eyes. After a year a
year today, a day that I should have
celebrated. It is my birthday and she

claimed that was my present. A little bit harsher than last years. I won't lie; I didn't know Jana after this year. She was fucking me exactly a year ago for my birthday and she thought it would be a great gift. Jana wasn't fucking me this year, but she still fucked an oblivious man.

I never knew you, you never knew me and you will never know yourself, I know that much.

Scared shitless

I was so frightened every time, every year. My mother would wake my sisters and me up to get around. I would be tired from a night of restless anxiety, one long anxiety attack. I remember how scared I would be when we would walk out to the car. The Texas morning heat already in full swing.

My mother would pull around with the rest of the house wives and wait in line. There would always be more people on the first day than the normal amount of traffic in front of the school. Most kids being escorted by their mothers. My mother would drop us off and immediately I lock up inside as I have to find my home room class to get to.

I would walk around confused, alone; these are the things I remember. The halls start to clear, the cars start to thin out and I would be walking around. After a minute or two of walking, feeling the nervousness build up as I would walk up to the big solid wood door, scared to turn the

knob. I had to though I had no choice.
Everybody turns and looks at the door
and the teacher stops and looks at me
angrily wondering who and why I was
late.

Some faces I would recognize and
most I had never met. There would
always be a squeaky chair towards the
front of the class and I would be told
to take a seat. I would sit down and
the kids would stare. I was taller than
most of the boy's by at least a couple,
but I was passive during these years.
These are the years my father would get
angry for me being a pussy. Smaller
boys would fuck with me and I would
allow them. Years later my dad had
received his wish, but he created a
monster inside me that he would come to
regret as I grew a thick skin. As a
young man though I was passive, it just
seemed easier.

The first day of school always had
that smell of new pencils being
sharpened, fresh paper, and chalk,
everything intensified on this
particular day of your whole year. I
would look around at the posters that
the teacher would hang on the walls.
It would look like what an inmate in a
jail cell would do, take something

boring and try to cover some of the depression up. It was awkward for me, never really fitting in, never possessing good social skills. The good thing was that I was never the kid crying to his mother, or the kid who would puke. For some reason there was someone who puked for the first couple of weeks then some under paid janitor would have to come in with the saw dust and clean some fucking kids puke up. I remember in first grade a kid spent the first week by the bathrooms, running in there dry heaving. After the first week the teacher told him that he had to control himself or go home.

Then there was lunch. For some reason lunch time would feel like, what years later I would come to know, a line to get your tray in a jail cell. I would get in line, grab my tray, pay for it and then look around quickly. I always ended up sitting alone as I didn't know who I was and clueless to what was going on. I would eat my bland meal, return my tray and go outside. I remember how big the playground seemed. It was big enough to hide from nothing. The Texas heat never scarred us as kids. I would see the teachers smoking in the corner of the shaded bench.

I wonder at times, when I remember this time of my life existed, what the old school looks and feels like. I do forget that this period in my life happened. I know it seems strange, but I've blocked out a lot worst in my life. I wonder if the halls are as big as I remember them. Does the gym still smell stale and did the lights still flicker, about only half working? Was the gym locker rooms still little rooms where I spent so many nervous minutes before a game? Somehow I could block out a crowd when a game would start, anything that I could concentrate on and forget about the spectators. I laugh when I think back, I laugh at me. Most kids didn't care, school was fun for them.

I did become friends with a boy who lived down the street. His name was Clint and he was from a small mountain town in California. We would ride our bikes through the large amounts of cement sidewalks and the playground. One day Clint and I found a way to break into the old gym. A few years later we were breaking in, smoking pot on the third floor that the school seem to forget about.

As a few years had passed we started to use this gym as a secret hideout and I started to grow and find the real me. Taking girls up there laying in the dark, happy to run my fingers down a girls spine feeling how soft and fragile she was, how interesting. We would let the morning turn to evening, laying there high on that feeling of truly holding a girl. The girls would leave and Clint and I would go out to the old football field. The school used it as a practice field and the track team and P.E. classes. Clint and I would stack up the big thick foam mats. We would climb on top of the highest point, the old coaches box and we would jump off having the time of our lives, like our summers, carefree.

I forget these years existed and for good reasons, but it is nice sometimes is funny to think of the Christmas plays, were I was a tree stump once for a Christmas tree. I would never want to relive these years but they are funny to look back on sometimes, reminding you how you developed, how you started to be who you became.

What you think you
Might want

It was really odd because I had seen
Tara a million times. I introduced her to my
friend, but Tara and I had a past, before my
friend even knew that Tara even existed. I
had the pleasure of knowing her during the
years that you explore and are young and
innocent. Our time had already come to a
halt long before, but that has nothing to do
with this story. In fact this whole
encounter that I am about to blab about has
more to do with what didn't happen, or never
even took place.

My friend and I had come in drunk and
happy to his home. Like I said I had
introduced Tara and him, all was good but
things still happened. Tara comes out when
we walk through the door and she is wearing
a nighty, or something along those lines. I
respect and even applaud their found love,
but she came out of the room like no woman I
had ever lived with and she was obviously
thinking that they were alone during that
incident. It seems normal to my friend, but
to me it was abnormal. Every woman that I
attempted to live with never came out
looking so different, passionate. It wasn't
Tara, even though she looked good, it was
the thought, of what I didn't get.

Maybe it was natural for Tara, although
I did not see that, or I had been shown the

other types instead? Life was good, but I was missing a true female companion, a muse, something to take my mind off of the normal bullshit of life. As I realize that maybe my life just lacks a little, I also realize that life does take more than what I was giving in.

So I go on the hunt. I decide to do the fun logical thing and just find a girl who wanted to skip town for a couple of days. Just smoke, drink, play my guitar with Brewtus at my feet and a girl to fuck. I find one; it was not hard because what girl doesn't want a free trip out of town. She is pretty and becomes attached quickly. I lay with her naked, cold breeze coming through the window, she kisses me lightly and I let her know that I am there. Later she felt guilty, so I'm not sure if I'll get a weekend fling to clear my head. When in need of ignoring life's problems, just go out of town for a few days and fuck another lost soul.

She makes me feel like it's raining outside

Sometimes I wonder if someone up there will find me. I walk alone, spirits broken.

Streets always empty. Will somebody find me, do I walk alone.

She left me on a sunny day. Some days the air feels as cold as the night. I didn't want to go and she didn't want to wait.

She depresses me when she was here and depresses me now that she is gone. Who knows what love is? I'm always lonesome when she was with me, yet I let my mind get me.

Lost and alone is what I have become, rainy day parades, she told me it was right, sick of her fucking up my life.

It's somebody else now. What and where did it go wrong?

When will the next go wrong, or right?

Would my mother approve?

I light a joint, finish, light a
cigarette and take a pull from Mr.
Walker...

I didn't know her name, it's been two
days and she's just one...

I take a hand full of these little
white pills and wash them down with a
twelve pack of beer...

I haven't called on mother's day or
birthday's, what day is it?

But don't leave me in the ground alone,
no matter what I've done. I still
demand...

A life falling, needing to stay awake,
or asleep? Myself and me, that's the
difference, now needing out...

Too many skeletons's, too much built
up, undeniable pain to come, a promised
twinge...

Pain that I've promised myself long ago.

Do I achieve? Did I achieve?

When you become satisfied, you begin to die...........................

80 oz's from where I need to be

I'm trying to sleep. I stay awake during the nights when most people are sleeping. I find comfort in not having to participate with the rest of the world in the traditional sense of a traditional day.

So here it is four in the afternoon and I can't sleep. I black my windows out yet light haunts its way in. I get up and stretch. I have a bad back due to being a work mule for too long. I want to write a great story, but I am incapable of doing this simple task. I turn on the record player and light a cigarette; I start to think as I hear cars in a hurry going where?

The phone rings. "Mike, I'm surprised you picked up." "Me too." "We'll I'll let you get back to sleep." I went along with her thinking I was asleep. I didn't feel like talking. My apartment has become stale. The look of it is pathetic, no excuses. It's your

classic junky living arrangements.
Countless beer cans, whiskey bottles,
wine bottles, a floor worse than a
theaters, and shit scattered,
cigarettes burns, over flowing
ashtrays. I head for the door and grab
my jacket

The streets are full of people. I
was broke, just a couple of dollars
literally. I walk past rich people
sitting in the warm restaurants eating,
smiling, and having someone there with
them. I grab a hot dog and sit at the
park bench. I eat half and give the
other half to my dog. I watch as people
walk. They move over a few steps
assuming my dog is mean when he is like
a teddy bear in all reality. Everybody
seems to have someone and they all seem
to be smiling, really happy. This is
some of the reason why I don't like to
go out in the daytime. I like to sit,
smoke, drink, and walk the late night
streets, the time during the drifters,
loners, weirdoes, and the never ending
scum known as whores.

The liquor store was around the
corner. I tied my dog off in front and
go in and bought to fourtys. The
cheapest shit they had, needing as much
as I could get with pocket change. I

count the change out and head out of the little store that smelt like shit. My dog and I start to walk back and a whore approached me. Prostitution was everywhere, anytime. "I'm sorry sweetie; I had barely enough to buy these fourtys." She is gorgeous and the thought of not being alone for a couple hours sounded so good, but not that way. She doesn't believe me; she doesn't believe I'm broke.

I always leave my cell phone at home and checked it when I returned to my shithole of a flat. One text message was on there, "Good night my love." Less than twelve hours ago this girl broke it off with me and then a message like that from her pops up. I take my little white pills and down eighty oz's of beer and pass out. I couldn't be toyed with. She was mind fucking me and I kept letting her. She broke it off then wanted to come back, so I remind her she broke it off with me when she decided to call and check on me at that moment. I told her before hanging up and passing out, that I loved her and I meant it, I just couldn't be with her. It has been my experience that most women will not take these answers and let it be, but she did and that made me wonder. It made me wonder if there was somebody else in her shadows, or was she the only mature girl that has seen through my bullshit. Either way I feel remorse, for being me, for being broke, for spending my last bit of money on 80 oz of freedom.

I like to hear
A little guitar

The sweet smell of rain coming through the
windows on this early morning. Most mornings
I get up and do my routine. This morning was
different, but still like so many. I didn't
want to listen to music, or watch the idiot
box; instead I made a pot of coffee and
rolled up a blunt. I drank a couple cups of
coffee while I smoked and listen to the
rain. The silence outside, but the noise
from the rain, made me smile. I could hear
soft decent music playing inside my head.
     I was enjoying the pleasant feeling
that I was beginning to feel. Maybe I was
relaxed? I drink another cup of coffee and
smoke a couple of cigarettes while listening
to the rain. The rain was turning, from
light to heavy. It was almost like a light
tribal beat. I went inside to grab my
acoustic and my harmonica, and then went
back out onto the porch. I didn't want to
hear my weak voice, so I only played along
with the rain. It was so nice; it was like
the rain was singing for me. Being outside
made the guitar sound great and the
harmonica seemed a bit sweeter. The best
thing about this morning particular was the
fact that it really was a care free day. No
phone calls, visitor's, and no fucking work.
Just the sound of rain, the harp and a
little guitar.

A bum note

I had been looking forward to
going to watch one of my favorite bands
for a few weeks. I had asked a girl to
go and this was going to be our first
date, our first time out away from all
our mutual friends. I was actually
excited as it got down to the final
week countdown. I went and got a
haircut, cleaned my car and made sure
my bank role was full. I call to
confirm our date and I got her
voicemail. I leave a message just
saying to give me a call when she got
the time. She never returned my call
that evening.

The next morning I see I had
received a message through the night.
I knew that it was her and I listen to
it not wanting to. She was copping out
on me on the last minute. I'm not sure
why I was excited about this particular
girl, she was really nobody to me, but
I had let myself get over worked about
the date. I headed to the concert alone

depressed, just wanting somebody there with me, maybe just a conversation?

I stopped at a bar not too far from the venue that I was headed to and decided to get a drink, maybe find a lost soul to go with me. The bar looked nice from the outside and then I walk in and it had mildew, musky smell to it. It was dim in there though and a mixed crowd, so I felt comfortable with the atmosphere. There was a circle of people who were headed to the same concert that I was. They had drove from Louisiana and was trying to buy tickets for a couple of friends who at the last minute wanted to go. There was a beautiful blonde with them who kept staring at me. She didn't talk much, which I liked, mysterious like me.

Her name is not important, but she starts talking to me, pulling herself closer to talk over the music in the background. The group of friends start to pile into their SUV, after I finally was able to talk to her, so that they could make it to the show early enough to find tickets. I looked at the guy driving and told him to take my tickets. "How much do I owe you," he says as he takes them from my hand. "Nothing man. Maybe you can have the night I wanted to have." He takes them and thanks me about twenty times and I tell him that it was my pleasure.

"Mike," is what I heard as I walk back to my car. I turn and it's the beautiful blonde. I wave and turn back towards my car. She comes running up and asked if she could go with me. "You should stay with your friends." Her friends pull away and I asked her what she was doing, what she would do if I was to say no. "I would take a cab I guess," is what she replies. I told her to get in the car and she makes it clear she wants to fuck. I get a room downtown Dallas and we fuck all night, like she was a goddess of the fuck your brains out. We snorted some blow she had and kept on going. I finally crashed and fell asleep with her in my arms.

I wake around ten am and she is nowhere to be found, not a trace of her. She left a note saying she loved me and maybe our paths would cross again in a weird way. She said that she hoped so.

I don't really know if she really existed, but I know I couldn't be alone with myself, loneliness would have killed me that night.

Cool to ignore?

"Mike let's hit the bar." This is what I hear all the time. I do hit the bars, but I like to go alone. An entourage was never my style.

"Come on, let's go get some pussy. What the fuck else you going to do?" Why would I want to go out with a bunch of dudes to get pussy?" They finally leave me alone knowing I'm a loner and not a leech. I get drunk and start buying rounds.

So I venture out by myself. I sit in the dark corners writing about the locals. One man is asleep in the other dark corner. He is snoring loud and was obviously intoxicated. The bar manager doesn't seem to mind. They could get a fine, but I have a feeling that they don't get hassled. I drink my whiskey with a beer chaser. People start to trickle in. The university was down the road, so little groups of girls and little groups of guys would come in and check out the vibe.

A group of college girls come in.
I see one eyeballing me from the bar.
She squints not being able to really
see me. The girls start playing pool at
the nearest table to me. I smell their
sweet perfume in a stale sweaty
smelling bar. I see the one they called
Josie, eyeballing me again. I light a
cigarette and look back every once in a
while, then look away, not smiling
once.

I get up to get a beer and walked
pass the table smiling at all the girls
and you could feel Josie starring
through me. I walk back by, not looking
and go to my dark haven. I pull the get
up and get a beer a couple more times.
The whole key is to be mysterious, but
you have to do it right. For instance,
Josie was with a group of girls. This
meant that all it took was one girl to
say let's go, usually the bitter one of
the group, the bitch. You gauge the
amount of fun they are having. As long
as they are having fun, they will stay.

I see my opportunity to pull my,
"move," the right time. I see Josie go
to the restroom near the bar. I go to
the bar to pay up and she walks out. I
see big beautiful blue eyes staring at
me, so I look down. I step out in front

of her acting like I stepped out without looking. "Sorry, I should watch where I'm going."

I look in her eyes and smile knowing that's what she needed to initiate the conversation. Most of the time they ask about my tattoos being an easy conversation starter. Every girl like Josie never actually look at tattoos, they just like the novelty. As a weak man I use my passions to hook them. I listen to her talk, and then the bitch friend always wants to leave always when you finally start to get to know the girl. "I can give you a ride." Josie takes my offer not wanting to end the conversation yet, or so called conversation.

A woman with big fake tits will use that gift to step on honest tittyless people. They use them in everything, epically on stupid men. For a man it's about your stature. Money, houses, cars, novelties, your job, all these are what us as men use as our leverage.

Josie ask about me and I tell her what I know so I won't have to drop her off in a bit, no I tell her what I know will get her to my house. "I play

guitar in a band, I'm a published
author, and I own my own company." Then
I hooked her. "I would love to read
some of your work, maybe you can play a
little guitar for me." That's why I
don't need any fucking entourage.
That's being a pussy

Destitute

Eye's through the soul? But the eye's
never lied.

Looking and looking, but never
understood

What was wrong?

Why couldn't it work?

Forgetting something, something unknown

Lacking something, we need to be told.

Going on, nowhere, anywhere to be
found, nothing to be said, bad dreams
when we went to bed.

    All the masse's always said that
    something was lacking in my head

Don't tell me don't

The other day, I was driving down
the road, when my friend Lou called me.
I hadn't seen Lou in a long time and
was excited about hanging out with him;
drink a couple of cold ones. "Mike it's
good to hear your voice and can't wait
to see you", Lou told me this a week
before arriving in Dallas. I stocked up
on liquor, bought some steaks and
bought a sack of hydro.

I see Lou walking towards me,
smiling, but he looked different. "Hey
Lou, how the fuck you been you son of a
bitch". "I'm doing good Mike, very
well". Lou had this weird happy look
stuck on his face. We drive back to my
house, while Lou talks in a pleasant
yet monotone voice and he smiles the
whole time. Lou then dives into the
subject of God. He had said that he
found God two years ago. I
congratulated him, not knowing how to
answer that. We arrive at my house and
I turned on the record player then
popped open a beer. I offer Lou one and

he refuses. Lou keeps talking, so I roll up a blunt, lit it, then asked if he would like any. Lou declines, but I didn't care because it was more for me.

"Mike have you ever thought that maybe there is emptiness in your life somewhere?" "No Lou, I'm feeling pretty good these days. Too much going on, never enough time." "Mike did you ever think that if you don't do the things that you do, that life might be less stressful on you". "I don't know Lou; this blunt is relaxing me pretty good. Is there some point you're trying to get to?" "I just don't believe you should be doing the things that you do, you're smarter than this Mike". I went insane. I looked at my house, my truck, and my books and started to get angry with Lou. My depression, anger, passions, they are what got me where I am today.

"Look Lou, take a cab and go stay at a motel". "What Mike? "Lou you crossed my line, you disrespected me. What gives you the right to come to my home and give me a fucking lecture on life? You are the one in denial, walking around with a smile on your face that looks like it hurt to put it on. Lou you ever have problems, or are you superman"?

A person can never tell me, "Don't do this or that". This is my one and only life I'll ever have a shot at. I don't need someone else's manual on life.

Earn

Just another Friday, I thought to
myself as I rolled out of bed. I had
to get up and find a friend to lone me
some money. I needed cigarettes and
some booze. I served in Nam and this
was the life I lived.

I walked into the dive beside my
room I rented for one hundred dollars a
week, a piece of shit room. "Hey Ernie,
how are you today?" I mumbled hello as
I walked into the darkness of the bar,
it helped clear my head. "Hey Hal, you
think I can get one on the house?" "I
don't know Ernie; your tab is getting
up there." Mike walked in, a local
drunkard. Mike had sold a couple of
books and had some money, most of it
Mike blew on booze, women, weed and
sometimes other things.

"Hey Mike." "Hey Ernie how are?"
Mike was young, but could out drink
anybody in that sad black hole. "Hey
Mike you think you could lone me thirty
bucks? The government is late on my
check and I need some supplies." "How

about I buy you a pack of smokes and a fifth?" That was the best I was going to do. I served my country, saw things people shouldn't see, was crippled for life, mind and body. So this was life, begging, owing, slumming, this was all I know now.

Mike and I walk down the street to the corner liquor store. "Sorry about your check Ernie, but I have to watch my money until my next check from my book." "Thanks Mike, I just want to die. I never understood why I lived through the war. I've been isolated for years, waking up not knowing what went on the night before, just drinking myself stupid." "I can relate to that Ernie." I knew he couldn't, but I needed that booze and smokes. Mike goes in and gets me a pack and a fifth, both cheapest that the store had. "Here Ernie, I got to go." Mike was always darting out the door no matter what the situation was. Anytime someone talked to him for a few minutes he left. Mike was weird, tattoos everywhere, bearded, always wearing sunglasses and always writing, thinking. Either way the young fucker helped me through another day that I was cursed to suffer through. Who the fuck knows what I'll do in the

morning? I guess I'll go drown my
sorrow and hope that my check is in the
mail in the morning.

I left straight for the war and
they can't even give me what I earned
without making me wait

An Introverted outlook
In this extroverted world

I awoke this morning, off of the floor, feeling like shit. It's the third time this month that this has happened. No these was not from a fun night out of drinking and think less acts, no this was something I couldn't quite get figured out. Life had definitely been getting to me. One night I woke with my best friend licking my face. Brutus my Boxer had found me on the bathroom floor. Other people seem to be handling this mess of a world better than I was; I was having a hard time just processing everyday behavior.

The world perceived me as a confident, young, good looking and an achiever. This is what I was against, the weight of the world. Not literally just mentally. Why do these people think that I am weird when they are the weird one, the outcast? If we could just meet at a middle ground somewhere.

I conquer whatever they throw at me, but the people throwing were swine, so it was a never ending battle, us and them. I smile and wave, play their game, take their money as they take my precious time. I guess we counteract each other?

They say that introverted people wouldn't be able to truly function without extroverted people. The problem is the introverted people and I am outnumbered.

Give me a piece of paper, she finally threw me away

Friendship is and always rare,
    I grew to be quite fond,
    but it was normal.

I read between the lines thought,
    listening to everything I've been
told,
    When will I learn? Can I learn?
                                    A
beautiful soul, just throwing me away,
I became everything to nothing for her.
    I'm at least going to be alone,
not by choice; everything was so inane,
and insecure. To her though, I'm worth
less than this piece of paper.

So I turn this piece of paper over and
write a poem, a poem of my love and
confusion I had developed for my mean
muse.

    I write it in the parking lot of a
gas station. I write of the beauty of
her, the beauty of our short
relationship.

I normally write out of anger towards women, but I could find nothing but love for my mean muse.

I finish writing about us and wad the paper up. I go into the store and throw it away in the trash can by the door. I get a beer and smokes and feel like I threw her away to.

Not only did she throw me away, but I feel like what I wrote and waded up was me throwing us away for good

Hidden cracks that
Don't show

She lived with her head in the clouds,
Refusing to ever look around.
So much goes unnoticed when you refuse to look up,
So much hidden in the cracks alone,
How will it change?
This is just a mutiny of denial, no responsibility taken,
Only given.
People must finish what they start,
What happens when they keep trying to hide the truth in the
cracks of society?
The streets will over flow with sewage, people, rats,
Pure chaos will prevail.
This is what people choose, I'm watching, waiting.
Not sure what the wait is for, but the more stuff that is brought
out daily tells me that you can't hide the truth anymore.
I'm going to smoke this cigarette and drink this beer
And try not to lend a hand to these people.

Life is too short to be hidden in the cracks.

How long will you stay with me?

"Mike you're an asshole," Heather yells at me. "What the fuck do you expect, you always stick around, and nobody is putting a gun to your head." I admit that I am a chicken shit when it comes to women. I always feel like one day they'll go, if I just stay silent. I become infatuated with these women and like everybody else; I enjoy the freshness of a relationship. That's why relationships fall apart in my opinion. What do I know about love though? "What do I know you fucking whore?"

So I sit and take the mental abuse, my comfort zone. When I talk to Heather, I am mean and straight to the point. I want her to know that I am tired of her. I can't be a mature man about it. No I just push her away, just like the ones before Heather and the ones after. That is always my plan though, anything is better than nothing. Heather has become a distraction to me and this causes me

not to function well, but I do what I
have to do to make it through the day.
"Heather just go. You don't need me and
I don't need you. It's been fun at
times, but times for you, your friends
and their opinions to go." That's what
I wish I could say to her, but I stay
silent, eventually the day will come,
until then I'll just look over my
shoulder.

"I'm gone, you can kiss my ass
goodbye," Heather yells after about
three months of putting up with me. I
really did hate to see that sweet piece
of ass leave. She was that and I was
what I was. I could never even begin to
grow to love someone like her. Some
things you say that you can't get back.
A person can try their hardest to
change the truth, but drunken rages
bring out the truth in most women. I
was not a mad drunk. No I make it where
the women have to be remorseful. They
always call, apologizing, trying to get
me to answer my phone. I admit that at
times I would love to pick up and
scream sometimes, lie at other times,
but I just simply didn't feel the need
for the headache. I've seen whores fuck
beer bottles, so I know there are women

out there who will take it and go about
their business.

I love a woman who comes with directions

I love woman. Each woman is unique in their own little way. That's why I love women and then of course the obvious reason. I can't help myself, wondering what all these women passing by me, what they look like naked, how they fuck, even what they are sporting underneath. I love the conservative type, the crazy type and everything in between. Most women like me when they get to know me, but their initial impression of me is usually not that good. I've learned that you really can't judge a book by its cover, that's why I believe women all have something different, good, but different about themselves. "Women are difficult, shit, all women are high maintenance", is what I hear from friends, but these people love drama not passion. It would be easier if every woman came with a set of directions, but they don't. This may be a problem for some. A typical male will not stop to ask for directions, me on the other hand, I don't mind to stop and ask for directions.

I'd disappoint you to

She looks at me with such beauty
in her eyes. This is just a distant
memory though. I'm afraid I've
disappointed to many, burnt to many
bridges. I remember my innocent loves
and how they were the chain of many
reoccurring incidents. I still try, I
attempt every time, but I am who I am,
so I can't really make any excuses, but
I try.

I let one in; I'll let her make me
and herself happy before I do what I
do.

I love the feeling of fresh love
making, the curiosity. A woman will
start too really like me and waste my
time, but then I disappoint them. I
guess I'm not what they expected. I'm
assuming that's what the problem is. I
stay busy though to keep my mind from
wondering off. This morning, I went
through my daily routine of getting
some coffee. The cute girl behind the
counter had always struck up a

conversation with me ever since I gave
her a copy of one of my collections. I
imagine what she is wearing underneath,
or what she tastes like when you kiss
her on the neck. I sit down with my
coffee and start to read the paper. The
paper disappoints me and I find myself
distracted by the cutie working.

"So Mike how have you been? I
haven't seen you in a couple of weeks".
"I just got back from traveling and I'm
bored with life at the moment". She
laughs and I tell her I like the way
she laughs. "Why?" She would ask me. I
told her it was cute like her. I do get
bored, not knowing what she wants me to
say. She hands me her number as I tell
her bye and get up and walk out. I look
at it and smile. It's a comforting
feeling, reminds me. So I take the
number, I'll call the number and I'm
sure I'll forget in due time that the
number will be forgotten, lost, some
sort of bullshit that I will probably
pull.

I wonder what she is wearing
underneath her tight jeans. Maybe I'll
keep the number for awhile.

If I went with you

I think I am beginning to love her. Her name is Tabitha and she is gorgeous. I met Tabitha at the wrong time in my life. We made it a great time, just the wrong time. I still cannot shake Tabitha from my head. She gave me much grief and somehow it doesn't, it didn't bother me. I know that it bothers her, but I believe she enjoys it.

I decided that even though it was wrong, I wanted to be alone with her. We laid naked, drinking, smoking, fucking and of course listening to my records. Tabitha asked me if I would like to leave town with her. "I can't, I have plans, but I would love to." "You just don't want to spend time with me." She couldn't have been more wrong. I wanted to go away; I wanted to fuck her for a few days, alone, never even wearing clothes until we left. I couldn't leave with her; I knew it would be wrong. Tabitha is too sweet and fragile and I am mean and hard.

"If I went with you, you wouldn't like me anymore." "FUCK YOU Mike, that's a cop out." "Your probably right babe." We would never last out in the real world, just depending on each other, nobody else. It was different me being gone traveling, gigging than to be around her all the time.

Tabitha hated me being gone. "You probably fuck everything that moves." I don't but sometimes want to, besides how do I know she doesn't fuck me over. Her insecurity drove her away from me. I drove her away, maybe she drove herself away from what could have been fanatical.

I'm not the one starring
At me

    Opinions that I don't want to know.
"Come on Mike, they'll only be over a few
hours. You never let my friends come over".
"I don't know Jana; you know people who
annoy me, especially when they are in my
house". It was pointless though, she doesn't
admit, but she always, always gets what she
wants. For some reason I'm fine with this.
I'm just a useless writer and Jana had a
great job. Most of the time she stayed at my
house, even though her place was much nicer.
I don't like staying at other people's
house. I had bought an old, decent house
with some money I saved when I sold a couple
songs and articles. Other than that, people
didn't seem to take an interest in my
writings. For some reason I'm fine with
this.

    The people who have humored me and
bought some of my writings and music, they
look at me like I'm weird. They look at me
now like I'm fucked up in the head. For some
reason I'm fine with this.

    Maybe this is why I like to be alone.
Drinking, smoking, these things are best
done alone. A person can enjoy those things
better and plus you don't have to worry
about me or anybody else acting like a
jackass. Other people around isn't too bad
in small doses. For some reason I'm fine
with that.

    Jana's friends show up and I can't tell
one from the other. They all look and sound
alike. I play along for a bit, drinking and

listening to them and answering certain questions they had for me. "Mike why are you able to travel a lot? What's it like to be a writer"? "Well Johnny, I'm not much of writer. I write things down and some people enjoy it. Jana did and fucked me". Johnny looks at me with an odd expression and asked me what I did before writing. "Well Johnny, I'm boring, what the fuck do you do?" Johnny proceeded to tell me that he was a banker. "Don't worry Johnny, its okay. It takes more than one type person to make the world turn." He begins to tell me something and I get up and go into the kitchen. I fill my glass to the top with pinot. I gulp it down and decided to go upstairs. I close my doors and roll up a blunt. I turn on my vinyl, light up the blunt and wonder why those people were so curious about me. They wanted to know why so many tattoos, or why my beard was so bushy. I opened the door to listen and they were all talking about their stupid opinions and outlooks on life.

    I stumble down the stairs, drunk, in my boxer's and no shame. I stand in the middle of them and over talk them. I yell about how they were all opinionated, dim-witted people." They were all staring at me and I continued, "don't look at me and think you know me, just look at the chicken heart in every man. I pull my nut sack out and put them over my pant waist line. It looks like a chicken heart. They all gasp, some actually laughed, and I didn't care because I'm not the one starring at me. For some reason I'm fine with that. Save me, fuck me, kill me, save me.

Karma Happens

Hoping to the dead, the king is dead. This was the weird, yet truth of what I really felt a few years ago. I just thought we went down and down and down. I thought the American dream was dead and I had no idea what that was quite yet. Of course I wasn't really bleeding white at the time. White seems so clean and comfortable, home. For years I had forgotten what home felt like, the smell and warmth. To tell the truth, I'm not sure if I could tell you what that smell is really like. I imagine like the scent of something baking, not burning.

When you spent years in the shitter, you tend to grow bitter without really knowing it. It's not healthy, just what we do as humans. Fixing the problem would be easier, but that's not what we do, we take the hard road. Fucking up everything, this just becoming a common act among man. Stealing, beating people, a different couch every night, this is what happens to you. If you're smart, or lucky, than you can hopefully better yourself. People like me are always walking that fine line, but some gather enough self respect and do something with their lives.

You do one of the two, sink or swim. If you choose to float on, there is still a problem. You find yourself changing for what is considered the better, but life kicks you in the balls. This was very hard for a person like me to understand for a long time. My truck would break down; my girl would leave me, cutbacks at work, everything short of frogs dropping from the sky. I became so bitter that I became worried about my mind. Why was I trying so hard and losing an uphill battle. I never really understood during these years, no this was too much for me; I just rode it out, cursing along the way

Year's later lives seem to loosen its grip on my manhood. It still had its moments of pure shit, but becoming easier. I started to think of how fucked up it was when I went from living in a little car to a two story that I owned. I was listening to a CD, when the man said, "Karma payment plan." I knew then that this is what I had been through. I fucked you and karma fucked me.

Everybody wins. It might take awhile but life will get you sooner or later. You steal my guitar then you might pay for it in many ways for many years. I will see you soon.

Long days

I wake up at about two in the afternoon. I look over and see a woman lying next to me. "Hello, hello, are you awake?" At first she mumbles something, and then looks up at me. "Who are you," she asked me. I told her I didn't know and asked her to leave. I needed her to leave so I could get my head right.

I get up and take a shower and get dressed. I start walking down the sidewalk headed towards the bar. "Hello Mike," the pretty bartender, Amy said to me, and I wave back at her. I needed some booze in me to set me straight. I knew my body and after last night I knew only booze was my medication. After a couple of tall ones, I head back to my house. I ran out of money, so I go home to drink some red wine. The first bottle went quick and tasted great.

I decided to get my laptop out and type. I open the second bottle of red wine and drink it while typing a few pages for my new novel. I lean back in my chair and light a cigarette. I start to dream about the possibilities of being able to live my dream, my dream of writing and people reading my writings. It's a nice thought, but I had to go back to reality, which gives me shivers. Could somebody make me believe, could somebody take me away? I shut my computer down and lay on my lumpy bed lying on the ground, no box springs or frame.

I was bored and have been for some time. I've worked hard, but nobody owed me anything, nobody cared. I finish the second bottle of red wine and get up for a third bottle. I was starting to get somewhat drunk. I needed to be. I needed to be drunk to get me through this long pointless day, a day I have wasted. I hope tomorrow I will be productive; maybe it'll be the day I create something great. Maybe it'll be the day that I become known? Maybe it'll be the day I fail terribly, but I'm sure it will turn out to be just another chapter to the self pity saga known as my life. All I can do is take

one day after the fucking last day and
then the next. If there is a next day
that is. I forget sometimes that today
will never come again. Once it hits
midnight it ends forever. Tomorrow may
never make it past one minute after
midnight. This could be it. We can only
hope so.

Never sorry until it's gone

Men and our ways, it's really a fucking joke. Women being the innocent creatures that we prey on, that we harmlessly go after. It never ends that way though. There are many bad and good things about ending a relationship. First there is the option of a fresh piece of ass. The thought of new conversation, hoping it is good. Then there is the pure darkness of loneliness that women can cause men to go through, it regulates on their moods.

It never matters what a women looks like, they can always get laid, especially out of spite. That's usually the same time that a man's back burner girl bails on him as well. Women know this and use it as a tool against men and our obvious ways. It just always works out that way. Men start to go into a depressing state of mind. They start to believe that they fucked up and should have begged the woman to stay. We convince ourselves that there were no bad times, like there was nothing wrong with the relationship. It's called denial. Some men beg the women to come back to them. Those men usually end up back at square one. For other men though, we wait it out. We try to remember the bad with the good. We try not to think of who they are fucking, who they are looking at in that special way. Men are driven by a curse though and we are never sorry until it is ripped away from us.

It's no longer the time of our lives were we can show up at three am and everything be okay. At the age of twenty five, the girls have turned into when and now if you're not around, they could be fucking someone else. No longer has booty calling getting women wet, just shutting us foolish men down and our human instincts, a mystery. This isn't about a piece of ass at this point of our lives. It's about companionship and realizing this and having to live with the thought of them fucking somebody else, and the next one and so on.

Make sure you don't want what you have before you throw it away. Remember the bad so that you don't become weak. Life doesn't always give us a second

chance. We all talk about fate, but
that is all bullshit. You have one
life. When a chapter is over then move
to the next one in your book of life.
Remember actions and words can never be
taking back. Think before you speak or
act a certain way. Think hard, it's the
only life you have.

A normal day

This morning was a bit special, different from most. For one I was in a good mood, and two I was playing hooky from work. I stay to myself quite a bit, and then you only have to worry about one person this way, me. I'm not really sure why I was full of energy, joy. I called my girl, Faith over to my house. I'm a terrible boyfriend, for too many reasons. By no means do I come close to a traditional boyfriend. I love her in my odd way, probably a cop out on my part. Three quarters of the time I'm a pain in the ass. Today was different though, I was going to try and do more traditional acts performed by most boyfriends.

We were among the masses in the middle of the day, and made it through the crowds of shit. We go to the bookstore and buy maps of Europe, with a dream of moving there together one day. We hope the day is sooner than later, this place is getting to both of us. We ease the built up anger of the curse of this city's madness by buying maps and trips, then we wait. It's fun though, forgetting about work and dreaming of a different life, a tailor made life. Most people either never make it, or never want to, but this was our dream. Me writing, smoking in the coffee shops, writing songs, maybe even be happy? The writers dream? Less worries. Faith pursuing her dream, not worrying about time clocks.

We kicked around the travel section of the book store, sitting in the aisle, looking at all the places. This lasted for about an hour. After that we walked over to

a world market and bought wines, good wines
to celebrate life and our venture into a
normal day. Before starting on all the wine,
we decide to go eat, a Chinese bistro, good
food. We keep talking about our dream. I was
enjoying it, looking at her happy glow. I
know I'm not capable of being a traditional
boyfriend all the time, but I try for Faith.
In the book store she had bought a Kama
sutra book that I didn't know about, but I
saw her looking at it on the way back to my
house. I told her to pick some new moves;
this task did not take her long. We go at
it, perfect ending to a normal day. Faith
knew me to good and leaves before I get
impatient for no reason. I roll a blunt, pop
open a cold beer and sit at my desk. My
writing cave consist of pictures, empty beer
cans, empty wine bottles, paper, pens, a
laptop and my must have records. I fire the
blunt and laptop up and put on a record. I
sat there for a couple of minutes, puffing,
happy from the day, the normal day and
decided to write this soon to be memory, not
wanting to forget this normal day with Faith

Patience on a monument

    I wonder how much time people waste. People say, "Mike come watch the game," but this sounds like a waste of time. I wonder if people have all these temporarily solutions to human boredom. Time is a bitch from just about every angle. I feel like I'm always waiting. I'm not sure what I am waiting on, but it feels like I am waiting on something unknown. This making me anxious never holding out for what might be better.
    Who in this world is unable to think of wasting your only time? It will never be yesterday again and will never be like yesterday. You have to wait though, wait on a door to open? I admire those people with the patience of a monument. This theory just seems a boring way to wait on death.

You looked at me
I exist

    As I sit in my motel room watching the clock, watching the clock since I returned at 3am. I smoke a few and pour a few and make it to 5:45am. I am counting down the time, just enough time to eat and leave. I feel better than ever though, like a weight has been lifted. What do I care if my music was liked by any of the mass? My project band had gone to shit to quick. There was a time that the chemistry between the three of us that could have done something. I didn't need to be known, playing music was a passion and playing was quenching my thirst for music. I just wanted to live life.

    It took a trip and playing with my sanity to see what was right in front of me. My beautiful and understanding Angel and also my boy Brewtus supported that. I didn't like my job, but if I had to work, it might as well be a descent job. From my experience all jobs are a pain in the ass. I'll always have an old beat up acoustic guitar, pen and paper along with my curiosity. I love to sit and people watch and then right stories about these unknown people. Nothing set me apart or made me special, I just wish I personally could enjoy the sunset.

    It's probably a, "half pass six", as my new friend Ian would say, when my Angel with Brewtus pulls up at the airport on time. She looked at me and for the first time in a week, I felt like I existed. I see a woman happy to see me, love me, misses me, most surprising, she puts up with me.

I hug her and then hugged my boy. Being an introverted person who has put me into isolation to many times, I realized that I was no longer alone. I've always felt alone, not there, or here, just confused.

Sometimes people would humor me with small talk, but I had no face to them. Everything that I have been using in such negative ways, were really positive things that were used in a negative way. I may never marry and have children, but right then I had somebody who loved me and still let me do my thing, still supporting me mentally. Everything leading up to this has shown me that I am living life.

My stories may never be read or talked about and my music may never be heard, but I don't think this was bugging me anymore. I believe what was bugging me was I only loved when I was alone and the rest times I was looking for a way out. I am a drifter at heart and nobody should have to live their life around a person like me, my mind. I knew this and I did love my Angel, but she knew me she knew me and my fucked up mind. The ordinary, jobs, people, love, hate, passion, ups, downs, friends, family, depression, failure, success and just life scared me. She was looking in my eyes though and I knew I existed. I knew I could conquer those fears with that support that twinkle in her beautiful brown eyes.

Like cattle, with one slaughtering

I stand in line and pretend, like everybody else, that these airline officer's are regular people. "Next," says the man behind the booth, with the smell of onions seeming to come off his push broom mustache. He asked for my passport and asked why I was traveling. "I needed to get the fuck out of town for a couple of weeks, so Europe it was." "Was it business or pleaser?" I replied that it was my business because I was tired of being interrogated because of the way I look. "Come with me sir," is what I heard next.

I was still fucked up from the drinking and the pills. They take me way in the back; I had no idea this airport was even that big. Two large men take me back there and then there was a huge third one waiting on me. They tell me that they are going to look through my stuff, so I take both my backpacks and turn them over. Demo Cd's and papers go flying everywhere, along with my medications. They asked me if I was an artist and what all the meds were for. I respond by saying that they could look for their fucking selves. I hear a loud thump and go to my knees. I stand up and the original asshole asks me to strip. I tell him to get bent and I feel my rib crack, this making it hard to breath, let alone answer any question. They throw the shit down and said thank you, as they walk away. "How do I get to the exit?" They kept walking and I start to pick up my stuff. I

take some band stickers and stick them to
the metal chairs, doors, poles, anywhere I
could stick them that would piss them off.
I needed to piss, so I go to the corner and
pissed what seemed like a gallon of booze
and start to find my way out. I quickly
found the herd from the flight and rejoined.
     I was bent over as I walked, trying to
catch my or somebody's breath. I walk by and
see the assholes that abused a bit of their
authority, and they are laughing. I was
close to the exit, so I flew them a bird. I
dart out the door and hit another terminal's
train and seen them headed towards the exit.
"Fuck You," is what I yelled them still
being about fifty yards away and they are
still at full speed. The train starts to
take off and they get the driver conductor
to stop. I pry open the other side's door
and they shut behind me. I was hurting, but
had to make it to the next terminal where I
could seek refuge in my truck. They of
course had radio connection with other
guards who come out; meanwhile the others
were stuck on the train for another
terminal.
     I slow down not to be too suspicious,
but it was hard for me not to stick out.
"Excuse me sir, you are strongly advised to
come with us." "We'll I have to strongly
decline your offer and then I pulled an
Emmitt Smith on their ass and out ran them
enough to hide in the parking garage. I saw
road blocks being drug out, so I got in my
truck and hauled ass, just waiting for the
worst and I guess they couldn't do anything
anymore. Fucking airline pricks. Fuck them.
The airlines are forgetting that they needed
a bail out not to long ago. FUCK THEM AND

YOU IF YOU WORK AS A SLAVE FOR THAT SCAM!!!
But I still need a way out. I guess I will
see what they do next time.

Protégé of a dead man

"Everyday turns out to be a little bit more like Bukowski," was playing on a new Modest Mouse CD. I fell in love with two things that day one being the new album and the other being introduced to the name Charles Bukowski. The song struck a curiosity in my mind about this writer, who was he?

I went to the local bookstore and nothing, the clerk had never even heard of him, so I go to the next bookstore and nothing. Finally I came across an old copy of one of his old collections. I had found the copy in a bookstore in a small town over in the county over owned by a little old woman. The old bitch had heard of him and had actually read quite a bit. I use the term bitch in a joking manner being how she read a lot of the man's work. "You look like you'll enjoy his work."

I went home and started to read it. I wanted to drink and smoke. Reading his material will do that.

Maybe it was because then you were in
his state of mind then. I was a little
freaked out, feeling like this man and
me were too similar, with the exception
of our backgrounds being really far
apart. No I related to him on a
personal, different way. I found out he
had been dead for a few years and it
made me kind of sad. I know if Bukowsi
was to be alive and meet me I know he
wouldn't like me. I'm betting he
wouldn't have like my work, because I
write with passion and about life,
that's should be what writers are
writing and that's what he wrote. He
would have turned me away to, but I
understand that. Regardless of what I
think Bukowski would think of me, I
know he would drink with me. I'll never
have that chance for him to get drunk
and yell at me and my new generation's
ways, opposite of his in too many ways.
Still the work lives on and the stories
are still being found. I live my life
to much like him, carrying on his
legacy. At least in my mind.

Bukowski didn't influence this
part of my life, that's one of the
reasons I think he would have had a
drink with me. Both of us almost
wanting to live in misery, depression,

but that passion still burning our midnight oil. Staying up late, drinking, smoking, writing fucked up thoughts, listening to our favorite music. Experiencing what we write, but writing lies as well. Some lies to let out anger towards other people or lies to create something that becomes an achievement. A sense of pride, wanting to admit it or not, it was our true pride.

What do I know though? I keep writing and reading and drinking, smoking. Bukowski's writings always reach me, every time I read them. I am the living protégé of a dead man.

Screaming through my mind

Its late night's with whiskey, vinyl
playing in the background, the air full
of thick smoke

It's about being alone, a necessity to
achieve through this different journey
through life's path's

I scream, but the walls are too thick.
I am ignored and I ignore right back,
to quick

The vinyl has told its story so I
change the record and pour another
whiskey and light another cigarette

Its criticism from friends who read one
line, but never supporting thoughts
outside of their boxes, a sad thought
on its own truth

It's about choosing to wear your heart
on your sleeve

The release it gives you as the night
continues to inspire you, sometimes

depressing you, sometimes making you
laugh out loud

She tried, but couldn't

Jana wanted to believe in me so bad. The stories I wrote the poems and my lifestyle. I live like the artists who I admired. Jana tried to understand the music and the introverted world that I lived in, but she just couldn't.

Jana grew to hate herself because of me. So I tried hard to prove to a lot of people who doubted me like the way Jana was starting to. I thought my notion on life would work if I worked hard, the way I worked in the oilfields.

Jana stopped reading my material. I would be playing my acoustic and she began leaving the same room that she use to gaze at me with her blue eyes while I played. I worked hard to get my material picked up by publishers. I was convinced that if I could sell one of myself published books then everything would fix itself. They say money can't buy you happiness, but I would rather have a comfortable, not a greedy life, but comfortable and be unhappy than poor and miserable. The stress level would at least go down knowing you could pay the bills on time.

"I'm going, maybe I'll contact you in the future, maybe you won't want me to, but stay listed if so. I can't take it anymore Mike. I wish you luck, but I've waited three years and all you do is write, drink, smoke and keep yourself to yourself. I'm not sure if I love you anymore, or if I ever did you, but I'm sure you'll write something about our chapter in life, that's what you do? Some material is stories and some are hate filled memories. Bye."

This note was on my writing desk facing the canal. All of Jana's stuff was gone, all of it, meaning she didn't even want to come back to at least let me look into her beautiful blue eyes one more time. I did want to write about our chapter in life, but I wanted to write about the good times that those big blue eyes that had made me feel better, gazing at each other. I use to be jealous of other people when I would leave the room, afraid she would find a better set of eyes to gaze into.

I drove myself to that cold
letter, the room cold from the windows
facing the canal, starting to fill the
little apartment with a cool breeze,
airing out the stale smoke. I sat in
what was becoming a dark room as the
shadows moved across the room. I poured
vodka and lit a cigarette; I was headed
to my depression, my old best friend.
I couldn't write, just thinking, my
worst enemy, me. I finish my drink,
turn on a lamp, and grab my wallet and
key's. I was going to find me a Jana
for a night. Maybe a woman who is alone
at the bar like me, unhappy. Maybe she
would keep me from me and read some of
my material, intimacy never taken
place. Just two lonely people who can't
be alone for our unknown reason as we
talk through the night. Talk about
life, passions, and people, enough to
start to see the shadows start to move
in the opposite direction.

A cough and a fart

She was one of my demons. "Mike come over to this house. I'm watching my aunt's house why she is out of town," Naomi says. We were young so any chance we would get to be alone we would take full advantage of; it was such a nice feeling.

Our relationship was at the stage were my chance of getting laid was about fifty fifty, some reason Naomi was always worth it. Naomi was undamaged and so pure.

I show up that night about seven. I was happy to see her and Naomi had such a genuine look of happiness in her eyes. This was a couple of years before you heard the phrase, did you hear he fucked her, always heart breaking, almost one of the worst lines to be told to a man.

Naomi always tasted so good; like that she was a rare human. When I walked in she was barely wearing anything. I love the way women dress at

home, so simple yet sexy. We playfully
fought and ended up on the couch making
out. Those day's I didn't need that
little white pill, or that drink, Naomi
was my first of many drugs.

We laid there watching a movie. I
don't recall the name; I was too busy
playing with Naomi's body. The
situation was so simple yet it was the
greatest feeling in the world, sadly
though that feeling dies with our
innocence. Naomi's aunt had a pool that
meant at least some partial nudity.

I got naked and jumped right in.
Naomi was changing and I was getting a
hard-on. She came out in a two piece
with her hair pulled up. She tests the
water with her toe and I tell her the
water was perfect. As Naomi slides into
the pool I go towards her. I hold her
closer than anything that I've ever
held. She shivers a little and somehow
I manage to pull her even closer. We
don't swim, instead we hold each other
kissing in the moonlight, such passion,
such missed passion.

Naomi gives herself to me in the
silence, the moonlight, the sincerity.
We made love and then went back into
her aunt's house. We meet in the shower

and fuck again, the power of that passion. I towel her off and Naomi goes into the master bedroom and I put my clothes back on. I lie back on the couch and sit up when she comes walking down the dim lighted hallway. Naomi was wearing a little dolly shirt and little cheerleader shorts. She lays me back down and lies down beside me. I had turned on the radio. I kept the lighting low and the music soft. I wanted to keep Naomi in the mood. We just laid there staring at each other, there was no world outside.

I start to cough. I couldn't control the cough as we lied there. After about a minute of coughing I farted. The room seemed so silent. Naomi tries to act like she had fallen asleep neither one of us wanting to acknowledge the fart. Naomi start to laugh and she is having a hard time not laughing. I began to laugh as well, feeling the situation was alright, that I was going to lose her over a fart. We went to the bedroom after the laughter and wrap up with each other, I was sure she would forget about it. I thought she had forgiven my fart.

A couple of days later I show up at her parents' house to pick her up.

Like most of the time Naomi was not
ready yet, which put me in the awkward
situation of being alone with her quite
father. He was always watching
television and we always sat there in
silence. A commercial had come on and
it was two men ice fishing. On starts
to cough and his friend recommends
whatever the product they were pushing.
The friend tells his buddy that he was
alright, but kept coughing and falls
through the ice. Naomi's father burst
out laughing. This is a man that I have
never really even heard talk and he was
genuinely laughing out loud. Naomi had
let my fart slip.

Dreams are a joke

"You can be anything you want to be when you grow up Mike." I laugh when I think of how young and gullible I was and fear I still may be. When I grew to my teenage years, I was constantly knocked down a peg. "You think you're going to graduate and go out and grab the world by the short and curlys?" I had a teacher ask me that once. When I finally escaped my prison from this planet, I started to become an individual. Life suddenly becomes huge, everybody's ready for change. It felt like we were house cats dropped off in the wild.

It's hard at first, trying to figure this world out. You grow though or you die. Then one day you see everybody changing again. Everybody married, having children and wearing khakis. It's sad because all my friends turn into what I fear the most; it starts feeling like your drinking with your parents. "Somebody has to clean the toilet's," I'll hear some asshole say. "Trade checks with them then, you fucking prick," I'll ask them. Meanwhile I'm trying to hold on to the thoughts of my old dreams. My view has become somewhat distorted though and I have fallen into an uncomfortable, comfort zone.

I'm sure there are reasons why they call them dreams. The world, the mass needs dreamers. The mass try to keep me from my dreams, but for me it is at least a good hobby and a nice thought.

Sitting through

I sit here drunk, shaking my head once again. I nod in and out, the fault caused by pills and more pills. I act like I care, like I believe what they say. Sitting through mindless chatter everywhere I go. Maybe it's my disconnected mind? Still having to sit through this, once again.

Next thing you know it becomes every day, this feeling every morning, feeling like a punching bag. Sitting through, sober, boredom, with nothing ever there. Sitting through people talking shit, making pretty things ugly, misunderstood, sometimes a miss guided mind with too many opinions Not only the sitting, but the waiting is killing me. When and where will the next be made? Will I make it a next round?

This is life, at least which is what is told to me every day. Just sitting, waiting, hoping we're not just waiting on death, even though death lurks in our shadows, the mystery. Who really knows, the masses are told and they follow faithfully, so I raise my glass to no one. I raise it because I've got nowhere to be, but I still have to sit through all this.

Suburbanite demon with a cute ass

Amber was her name. I personally knew it, but everyone else knows it in a different more common way. We think of Satan as ten feet tall, big horns, claws and of course a pitchfork. That's no longer the form that he and his demons take anymore. Now he takes the form of a blonde, tight assed suburbanite.

Amber was my personal demon and she was an advocate of the devil himself. It's like a bad drug that you can't run from, that you don't want to run from. First it starts with a cute smile and beautiful eyes. In their younger years they create chaos all the time. Their dad thinks that he has an angel when he has a self created monster. It's bait for a dumbass like me though. I know it's a game, but I like some of the bullshit. I grow tired of it quickly though and go running to the next little blonde and start it all over again.

It's not sad just human nature. Amber and I kept in touch over the next few years. "Hey Mike how are you?" "I'm doing fine, busy, busy. I'm doing alright, just living life, catching what it's thrown at me. How's your boy friend?" "Eh, let's talk about meeting up for dinner; it's been a couple of months of shit with him."

"Name when and where." We have grown more mature. Less young demons in my arms these days. Amber is great though. She never ask about my past relationships or work, it just always seem to be a relaxing, nice time, always needed. You know, a little reality thrown into the mix. The games she use to play with me have now become life. Instead of having chaos from hidden sex, we now indulge in it. Relationships are no longer used as a way to piss off the other, no now there not even talked about. Amber will always be my demon, the thought in the back of my head, the thought of how she moved, tasted, fucked different, even the way she lyed in my arms. There will be suburbanite demons for all you people, if not already. These demons are fun, mean, and helps pass the time, but we'll always demean each other, but love each other in a outlandish way, even a little hate unnerved in there. Basically they bring you back with the passion you get from something simple as companionship. Some people need their drug all the time and some just need a fix every once in awhile.

Me, I need Amber to call. I can't sit up straight, but I need her, I wish she would give me a distress call and I would run to her. I would let her use me and leave, like they do, but I love her, maybe? I believe at times that she loves me. The way she talks to me as she emerges herself in my arms, my lucky arms. Amber started as my demon, but she has never been my enemy, now it's just life, but I love her.

Sweet beautiful nothing

I try to tell you in clever riddle, the
wrong thing is what I said

I can't get all the bad thoughts out of
my motorized head

She would change my feelings for one
sweet moment, a beautiful nothing

I could never stay away, I need that
moment, that easy fix, the drug that
makes it worth waking up and it always
takes away the pain

I give her love and she gives me love
for that moment to be more beautiful as
we become one, but in my life, nothing
to gain

We don't see the same picture, but we
can still come together, companionship,
passion, her sweet breath, her warm
skin, the taste of her, I wish she
would think of me when I was gone

I did her wrong, but I'll always love
you and I know you'll always love our
sweet beautiful nothing moments

I know that one day you miss those
sweet beautiful moments and they won't
be there to take advantage of

To spend the night in my arms

The day music died

The news anchorman came on the TV during a commercial brake and says, "Music is dead, more at nine". I get up and turn off the TV; I knew that what the masses considered music was indeed dead. There was no more intelligent music, just the same following to a downward spiral. I go to my recording room and decide to listen to my records. My friend Amy calls me and says, "hey Mike can I come over and get high? I just feel like smoking tonight." I tell her it's okay to drop by, even though normally I would prefer to sulk alone.

"Hey Mike, you doing alright, you sounded upset on the phone, you okay?" "Amy I will never be okay." She looks at me funny and starts to tell me of her previous night and I make it clear that I didn't care. "I'm sorry Amy, but you called me and this is what I'm doing right now." "You always sit around writing and listening to your stupid records." I tell her that pop music is dead and that I was happy. "Then what's wrong with you Mike? You hate the radio and big record companies." "Yes, but I am afraid that the masses will let the real music starve and die." "What? That's dumb Mike." I ask her to leave and told her that we don't need each other. "Leave me alone Amy, I'm never alright."

"Fuck You Mike and your music. You'll never be anything, your living in a dream. We'll I don't need you, whatever the fuck you are anyway." "Thank you for the compliment you soulless whore." "Mike hide behind your bullshit, it's what you are good at and I hate you for that." "I am what I am babe. So go fuck yourself, or better yet go fuck someone else."

"Is this about your stupid thoughts of your music?" "It is The Thought Experiment, besides I thought you were leaving, like right now. Go fuck yourself bitch, your one of so many." "You're going nowhere Mike and I don't want to be there when your music dies." "Me either." "What does that me? Does that mean you agree?" Get the fuck out of my house and go get fucked whore, I have shit more important than you, pretty much anything." "You'll regret it Mike." "Maybe your right, but it won't be regretting you. Maybe

somebody worthy, but not some whore
like you. I'm regretting and forgetting
you as we speak. I thought you were
leaving? I need to get together for our
gig, the band going nowhere as you put
it.

The last time

It's happening too much, down on a knee, not asking for this. I was coughing a bit of blood up again, stomach not right, head even worse. The doctor keeps telling me that the alcohol isn't any good for me, but I ignore him. Who really cares any way, not me?

I'm too many miles away from where I need to be and my meds are running low, it starts to worry me. I need to make it back to America long enough to get them and return before I turn inane again. I'm sitting in a shady alley coffee shop, the air full of sweet smoke, people look at me and I turn my head. Amsterdam air in the coffee shop clears my head and I walk to the streets and then catch a lung full of the sweetness from the fresh air from the recent rain. I make my way in the late night down the sidewalk.

I stop in at a small pub down the sidewalk after walking a bit and decide to have some beers maybe a laugh? I drink my beer and order another. After ordering a few more rounds, I decided to go for a late night walk in the breezy fresh air. I keep walking and come across the Magic Mushroom and decide to run in and get some shrooms. It probably was not a good idea for my rot gut, but I always felt like shit, so I might as well have some fun, a small escape. I eat the mushrooms and light up a cigarette and walk around looking for a store open. After an unknown time, I came across a small store. I grab a twelve pack, two packs of

cigarettes and a pack of papers. I go back
to my room and decide to write; I had all
the necessary element's to run all night. I
look out the window of my small room and
look out at the canal and roll up a joint
and blow smoke through the lamp watching it
being sucked through the open window, the
streets are surprisingly quite, a rarerity
that is almost unsettling. I smoke
cigarettes and joints one after the other,
while I write through the night. The beer
runs out so I go to the second floor vending
machine where the machine had a place for
people like me, beer, so I fill up and head
back to the room to write.
    I convince myself this is the last
time.

I pushed my fingers through your mouth

Your perfume fills the air;
    she sleeps, looking so peaceful,

I can't sleep, due to my insomnia,

So I wake her, her breath as sweet as
her smell,

"Wake baby."
    She wakes, always so beautiful, so
lovable. We start to fuck, we don't
make love, no we fuck.

    She began to moan telling me she
loves me, I don't respond, I just push
my fingers through her mouth as she
sucks them before going down on me.

    I start to fantasize about other
women, maybe others that might love me,
but my mind drifts more than I do.

    The next morning I'm gone. I'm
gone for her, for her good. I believe

in being selfish, it's the only safe
way to play life.

Yes life is just a game and you are my
little figuring's in a pawn for life's
passion's you poor unknown idiot's.

To drunk for bunks

"Mike come pick me up," my cousin would
tell me over the phone. I would come in from
the city and would pick him up just about
every Friday night. As soon as I arrived we
went to get pot and beer. "How you been
Mike? I wanted to see you and get fucked up
there, it's been a while, heard you was
hiding out." "Yeah man, these small towns
scare me too much, besides you graduate soon
and you can move up to the city." My cousin
did most of the talking for the night, just
the way I like it. I get tired of talking.

We went to a few houses that had some
stuff going on, but not much. I got a couple
of numbers from some chicks that I actually
wanted to call. I never remember what or
who's who, I just wing it. Every place that
we stopped at, we got more and more fucked
up. Nobody recognized me, but everybody was
friendly enough, but I'm always on guard.
Everybody was sharing whatever they had and
that was fun for all of us. We spent the
rest of the night testing the outer limits.

My cousin had his own room behind his
parent's house. It was an old storage
building, turned into a bedroom and a couple
of couches in it. To save space, my cousin
had bunk beds. We would come in stumbling,
during the early morning hours. I turn on
the radio and roll up a joint. We talked for
a couple of hours, rambling about anything
we could think of. Like all fun days, this
one was coming to an end. My cousin had
always slept on the bottom bunk and I would

crash out on the top bunk. When we drank my cousin pissed a lot and that's what he got up to do and I told him to turn the radio up. We both hated to stand in silence.

"You piss to fucking much grandma." I was teasing him as he got up to take a piss. I settled in, that comfort zone that you feel, a secure feeling when you feel the comfort of the mattress. My cousin turned around and gave me the finger and the bed suddenly caved in. The metal frames fell on top of me, giving me a slight concussion. He makes sure I'm okay and works his way towards the lights. My cousin turns the light on and we both laugh our asses off at the mess. The room was trashed, it had broken his dresser, couch, clothes everywhere, and the worst part was when the radio had broken. We pick the mattresses up and toss shit to the side to make a flat spot to lie. My head hurt like hell, but some music would have eased my mind. FUCKING BUNKS.

What's your favorite song?

Maybe we could lay awhile, listen to the traffic,

Everybody on their way to work as we lay there naked and warm, so cold outside.

She was sexy, she would always put's on a good record, a good record to fuck me good to.

We could hear the pops of the record and I would look into her eyes as she talked about life. Her life was interesting in a weird way.

The record would end and I would see her naked ass get up and change the vinyl.

She would change sides, naked, me starring the whole time, beautiful and then jumped into bed.

No more traffic interrupts the passion.

My favorite band plays in the
background and I convince myself I love
her.

We shut the world out, listen to the
records and decided not to talk, but
listen to the music and fuck.

Inside who's head?

I couldn't shake it, Naomi was in my
head. I believe she was there to play with
my thought's, I wasn't ready though, this
was evidently my mind trying to flee. I had
become absent minded on what she had told
me, she said her goodbyes on her way out the
door, the door of the rest of her life. Her
smile was just tears in disguise, her faced
lied when she smiled. Naomi was beautiful
when she really smiled, but heaven is for
conversation, hell is for conversation.

I'm told god is a place where you wait
the rest of your life. I wonder what became
of Naomi's mind, what went wrong? In my
dreams though she is alive, but your crying
as your mouth moves, I believe in your heart
there was a spark that screamed for a lover
to bring you happiness. In my dreams you're
alive, but you're crying though, and I loved
you. The dream makes me feel we are one in
the same, in your head you leave with our
shame, putting everything in place. I wait
on a miracle, but god is a place where some
holy spectacle stays, wishing my face was on
her cheek.

This is all is my head I fear, but the
vinyl plays in the back ground. I couldn't
hate her as she left, in fact I wish I could
have left it again, that's means she would
be here, never headed for her way out, not
by my will. At least this reminds me of what
I was, what I use to be, reminding me not to

forget. In a sad way, I hope I never forget
her. If she could be here now, I would
create more to remember.

The new memories would be different
from those that we had previously made. We
are now full blown adults. Some life lived,
some of life not lived but we had become
more intelligent over the years. Battles
fought and won and battles fought and lost.
Was she all I remembered, or had she
drastically changed? Have I drastically
changed for that matter?

Whose head am I in? I would never want
to go down that road again. Realizing I had
only the day that I am living, I realize
that life was too short to keep going down
the same road.

Yesterday was her
Tomorrow

She didn't have a lot to say that
night. This life for her never felt right.
She spent so much time thinking about what
she didn't do in the past that was something
that affected her present. Her heart should
have been filled with joy, when instead it
was filled with depression and sorrow.
Outdated sorrow

She would lay naked with me on my lumpy
mattress, saying that nothing changes except
life's scenery arrangements. The depression
I would get from listening to her, "What
if's," The sad part is that we are young and
there was a passion in the bed to enjoy
instead, but immediately turns cold when we
are done fulfilling our human aggression.
She made me feel as if we had lived the same
day for the last 25 years. Like fear had led
her slender, beautiful body around to where
we are now, here. This woman who had so much
life to give, a certain glow when she wasn't
thinking, when she just lived life. But she
had convinced herself that yesterday was her
tomorrow.

I lit both of us a couple of cigarettes
as we laid there and she would talk, she had
no problem talking, finding the negative in
everything. As shit spewed from her mouth, I
started to think about my own life.

I look at her beautiful body and look
into her gorgeous eyes and I get out of bed.

She asked me what I was doing, why was I getting dressed. I couldn't think of what to say for a couple of minutes as I finish my cigarette and find my clothes around the floor from her ripping them off. She had no idea what wasted time was, only a wasted mind. I had my own problems and no matter how gorgeous she really was, I couldn't let my mind go to waste.

I tell her I love her in my way and that I couldn't have my yesterday as my tomorrow. "What", she says with a confused look and I see her breast and ask myself the same thing. I light another cigarette and tell her I've got to go. "This is your house Mike." "I don't know what or where I'm going, but I have to give in and forget the past." She is so unpredictable.

I barley had anything and I tell her I'll be back in two days. I came back in a day and packed my truck up and left her forever while she was out of the house.

"Mike have you disappeared," was the message I had on my phone, but couldn't let her drag me down anymore, so I don't respond right away. When we were on my bed, I became scared. Sure I loved that feeling of passing time in the nude with a gorgeous girl, but I couldn't give in. Somewhere it went wrong. She said everything was alright, but she fucked up my life, I can't forget that plague that she unleashed on me. I didn't want to waste anymore time thinking about the past, the future, or even us. Good bye my love, but I'm going to kick fiercely at this world around me.

It's been a handful of years now and life is a bit better. It took too long to get over her, but the more I thought about

her, the more I was going against what I
last said to her. I don't want yesterday to
be my tomorrow. So I stay focused, everyday
being unpredictable. Perfect!

200 fucking cigarettes

It's three a.m. on a Wednesday morning. I've been up for two days writing. An old, "FRIEND," stopped by and he had some coke. "Come on Mike, for old time sake." What the fuck does that really mean?" Kaz knew my weakness though as I am recovering addict. People tell me once an addict always an addict. I'll agree with that statement.

Kaz knew if I was going to do some coke, that he was going to have to bust out with a lot. If I'm going to fuck up, I might as well do it right. I smell that distinctive smell that coke has, that captivating smell. I hoover the tutor over the first rail and snort it like my nose still worked right. It hits me and I need more.

Kaz sells me the rest and I go to my room and play a record. I pop open a beer and start chugging. For me beer and coke always went hand and hand. I move my laptop over sitting it on my glass top coffee table. I throw the bag down and cut it all up. I spend the next few hours that ended up turning into two days.

I would write a story of greatness achieved, greatness conquered. The days go by and night comes and I keep switching the records, each time doing another rail, my energy drink.

When writing I always have a cigarette hanging out of my mouth. It's an artist habit. When I do coke, I lit the next cigarette with the one I'm smoking. People are calling, but I can't answer because they'll know, they'll come get me, but I don't let paranoia set in. I try to stay focused. The cigarettes' burning to fast and the beer doesn't take any of the edge off. I roll a spliff laced with coke and take a break from writing. It helps and level's me out for about an hour. It's dark outside again.

I light the cigarette and write about a girl who has been suckered by the world. Am I part of the world? It seems so real but its lie's. I run out of coke and the messages have filled my phone with anger. Girls wanting to know what the fuck, bosses yelling, and a lonely day as I come down. I try to

sleep but the coke was still going
strong, so I get back to writing. I
change to Johnny Walker and start to
roll my own cigarettes. My hands could
not be still, too much to do.

Now it's three a.m. and I see
every mistake with my small room. The
paranoia sets in and I become scared.
I lit another cigarette and look out
the window. The early morning hours are
getting ready for the hot sun. I roll
another spliff and drink my JW. I start
to feel depressed, too depressed to go
on. I grab my pistol to clean it. My
hands couldn't sit still. I give my gun
a good cleaning.

I become tired, but I still can't
sleep as darkness creeps up again. I
never conquered better days, better
ways. I thought of all my friends, my
heroes who have taken themselves out of
play.

I write a great story of a man
gaining such stature from nothing. A
man who shows everybody he's better
even though he use to be nothing, a
blur. Everybody fears this man, but
they fear him out of respect. I lit
another cigarette as I read it and put
the cigarette in my ashtray. I take my

pistol and think about shooting myself
in the stomach. My luck would have it
another way though. I would live; I
live to face problems. Everything that
reminds me of her, of who I am, who I'm
not. I lit a cigarette as I leave the
hospital against the doctor's wishes.
When I finish that cigarette I lit
another one. I had to face another
fucking day. I guess it's a good thing
I'm a junky, excuse my addictions. They
still numbered my endless days

Alone all the time,
never alone

I can't take it anymore. This life
is getting to me. I stay in my room
most of the time, smoking, drinking,
and watching mindless, soulless
television. I hear the phone ring, but
stay in bed, my haven.

"Mike open the door, get out of
bed and open the door. It's been days."
"Just leave me alone," I tell her. I
don't want to talk, but I want to
answer the door. I finally hear her go
away, so I get up and fix a tall one.
I sit down in front of the record
player and turn it on. "I knew you were
in there Mike, open the door." I open
the door and I'm happy to see her face.
I tell her I love her, but I don't feel
good.

"How long have you been drinking?
Has it been days, is your stomach
okay?" I want to hold her, but I also
want to be left alone. I didn't lose
passion for her; I just lost passion

for life, to keep living. She sits next
to me and I have nothing to say. I wish
I could love somebody, maybe myself,
but on the other hand I don't think I
cared anymore. The depths of this
pathetic loneliness have set me apart
from the world.

I need you, I just don't want you.

Bed sheet writings

I was drunk and feeling alone. It was cold out and I didn't want to get out of bed. I had my vodka and my cigarettes, a pen, but no paper. I laid back and swallowed the remaining vodka, while the music played softly in the background. My mind started to race with ideas of stories to write.

I finally get up and look for some paper. I was so broke that I was using old manuscripts to print out new stories on the other side. I was out though, I had written quite a bit after being fired from my job after three years. I found a dark marker and lay back on my bed. I started to write all over my bed sheet, it wasn't like my home was going to be in a better homes magazine. I just continued to sacrifice my sheet with my writings.

The next night I had a woman friend over. She kept coming over to me and grabbing my cock. I was fucked up and just wanted to lay back and go to sleep. "What is all this Mike? What's

all this on your sheet?" "My writings,"
I told her. The nameless girl set on
the edge of my mattress. She looks down
and reads something I had wrote, and
then she looks back up at me. She gets
up and put's on her clothes, and then
walks out the door.

Don't let people you meet read
your writings, were her parting words.

Celebrating, Sir Bukowski style

I was having a good week for a change. My side business was doing well and my bonus was pretty good this week. "Mike where you going" a co worker had asked me. I told him I was taking the day off. It was still early, so I decided to get a thirty dollar bottle of pinot. I open the bottle and smell the sweet aroma, as the wine begins to unlock it's self. I polished the bottle off by noon and decided to stop in the cigar lounge. I had never been there, but decided to stop in and get me a good cigar, the way Bukowski wood do to accommodate the booze in celebration.

I walk into the lounge and the lounge was quite nice, a nice "Man Cave", right down to the big screen and leather chairs. I go into the cigar room and the owner Joe Comes in. Joe looked like he owned a cigar shop, short, dark hair, and built like a Mack truck. Joe starts talking about his love for tobacco and he knew his entire inventory. It was like a kid talking about his new toy. This man loved his job and I envied him. I wasn't going to let it get me down though.

I bought a twenty dollar cigar, some wraps and headed out the door. I stopped in at the liquor store and grab a twelve pack of some good imported beer. I get back to the house and strip to my underwear while cracking open a beer. I rolled a joint and watched the smoke swirl in the lamp light and drinking a few more beers. Then I light the cigar up and puffed away. I wondered how much Bukowski would probably be annoyed by me, maybe we were alike. Isolation, good party favors and writing, it was a good week.

I love the thought of Bukowski not liking me. I grew up loving that man. If I was able to go back and meet that man, the man who knew true life, I would buy him a fine bottle of wine and just listen, learn and not over stay my welcome.

Chocolate pies and blue skies

I'm not sure why it is when a man gets snubbed by women why we as men take shit from one woman, at least from one woman in our lives. There is just something about that one special fuck buddy that was captivating, maybe because of her free spirit that came out.

My fuck buddy's name was Court and she was gorgeous, driving men crazy. Court was always trying to get out of her parent's house and I was her haven so to speak. "Mike will you come pick me up? I'm about to lose my mind." "Sure I'll be there in twenty minutes." She always smelt so good and cheered me up. Court would get me out my house, away from me. We would get high and lay through the night never answering the phone, just wanting to be alone.

Court called a few days later and we went out for lunch, sat on the patio eating chocolate pies, smoking

cigarettes. Court and I went back to
the haven and fucked. After fucking for
awhile we listen to the radio and
decided to take a shower. She was so
sexy wet, beautiful eyes, always a must
for me, eyes that speak. We fuck in the
shower and get out and fucked again,
and then we lie down and spoke of funny
things keeping the mood easy going.

Court sat through the night with
me, keeping each other from slipping
into loneliness. I will always remember
Court as my blue skies and chocolate
pie girl as we had sat on that patio
laughing, enjoying the nice weather as
I looked into her eyes and she looked
back.

I wonder where she is now day's?

Cut this city

I hear the streets,
The walk of the unknown feet,
The smell coming through my open window,
The shouts and laughter.
I hear all this and I get confused,
It seem like everybody in the city had
somewhere to go,
All I had was this small room, this city.
All of its demons, angels, thieves,
junkies, poverty,
But it seems as if one single road divides
these.
This city has been my savior and my
falling,
It's hard to tear apart from the only thing
you know.
The streets call, so I go to it, I try
not to think,
But this is unreasonable, not even knowing
the reasons.
Some don't understand, I truly don't
You can't find the reason in a certain
city's sound, watching the world go around.
No, you have to cut yourself from this
city and your ways, if not yours than
somebody's ways.

Distorted View

You ever felt that passion that you couldn't run from? A beautiful woman who gets you caught up in the moment with her? The kicker of this has to do with that woman having issues as soon as you become intimate. You want to be nice and listen to her inner torture, but on the other hand you've got your own problems to deal with.

This woman whose name is Katy, who I met one night when she thought that her ex-boyfriend was breaking into her house. Katy's roommate and I had been friends for a couple of years and he lived two blocks away. Johnny called and asked if I would go and check on her.

I get in my truck and head over to their house with a baseball bat. I look around and told Katy that there was no sign of anybody and told her she was more than welcome to crash on my couch.

I could see passion in her eyes when I asked her, like she wanted to, it made me feel good but that look with her pretty brown eyes stuck with me in my head. Katy and I talked at her house the next day, we were hanging out with her roommates but decided to go to my house and drink, listen to my vinyl's and just talk until sun up. Katy left in the early morning hours; I lit up a joint and crashed for a couple of hours.

"Hey Mike I got your number from Grant, hope you don't mind, I was seeing if you could get me some weed." This was the message I got, being as how I never answer the phone on a number I don't know. I call her back and told her I had some. She shows up in thirty minutes alone.

"Hey Katy, how are you? Come in." I offer her a drink and we both have one and sit down. She starts talking and we are starting to get a bit tipsy. Katy offers to roll a joint and then she became a loose cannon. I could tell right away that she probably liked a little drama, maybe a bit of personal issues to. We sat though talking and drinking the hours away. I look up and she is given me the same look she gave

me a few days ago. I could tell she
wanted me and I'm pretty sure I had
that look on my face to. That look of
pure passion.

Katy start's to kiss me and I kiss
her back. She start's to take my shirt
off. "Are you sure you want to Katy?"
"Yes, I need this." So we did what the
human chemistry mystery does to people.

We lay in bed, watching the smoke
twirl in the light from the lamp after
the first time. I start to feel her
smooth legs up to her smooth pussy.
Katy was ready to get it on and so was
I. We fucked like it would be our last
time ever. We finish and lay on our
stomachs talking. "I have a boyfriend
Mike and I don't want you to think I'm
a whore." I laugh a little and tell
her what she wants to hear. I've heard
that so much that it seemed to be the
line that women used quite often.

We become friends quick and start
to hangout a lot. She becomes attached
and I find myself being in love with
her passion. I have to stay in my way's
though, my need to be alone most of the
time. I become an asshole after a few
months, yet I couldn't bring myself to
free her from my fucked up mind.

Sometimes I lay with her and the world
around is non existing and other times
it becomes what it creates.

Mud, blood and snot

IT's 2 a.m. and Lee, Rockstar and I are baked. I wonder what the men who pick up the trash, what they think about the bags of empty beer cans. The three of us had been drinking since 11 a.m. and we were a bit jolly as well. We all smoke like we would stop breathing if we stopped smoking. I turn the air purifier on in the recording room and we sat in there playing our acoustic guitars.

The beer is still flowing, trying to kill the last case. I fire up a blunt and we play our guitars as that sweet skunky aroma fills the room before dying at the hand of the purifier.

I get the levels on the mic right and we start to play. We goof around, laughing at the mistakes, some of the songs and some good original shit. The originals just pop up during the fuck off shit, nothing's forced. We all three set our guitars down and smoke a bowl. "You know what fun is? Playing

house parties." Lee say's as we talk of
good times that we have had.

"I was playing a house party last
Halloween," I go into a story as we
smoked. "Yeah we were finished with our
last set, standing around talking to
the pussy that got wet from us playing.
We hadn't loaded the equipment yet,
just kicking it with the people and
they talked to us about music, how they
did this or that. All of them full of
shit, but they liked us.

Some of the fellows attending the
party didn't like the girl's giving us
so much attention, but what did they
expect. For some reason I always
attract trouble at functions. I'm a
quite, sit in the dark go with the flow
guy. So I start to talk to a little
hotty and this little guy named Kyle
comes up to me." "You got a problem
MOTHER FUCKER?" "I looked around and
Kyle was staring at me. I tell him we
can take it to the street." "I'll do it
right now, I don't need the street" he
says to me getting a little closer to
me. "Well I take that as a threat. I
hit a mother fucker who threatens me,"
so I drop his ass with a solid left and
bust his nose. His eyes tear up so I
kick the shit out of him and then throw

him in mud as blood and snot run down his shirt as everybody observes the bullshit talking hillbilly get beat.

Everyone backs up in silence as we load our equipment, as we watched each other's back. Other than that little problem, most house parties are great.

We laugh and exchange stories for about an hour when returning to the house, still drinking. Barely being able to sit up we grab our guitars, they seem to balance us in our seats. We play a song worthy of being recorded. Maybe it was the beer, the smoke, us being tired, but we all zoned out and just played. We had a great song recorded and had no idea what to call it, our minds being on their last minutes. "Mud Blood and Snot," Rockstar says" "Sounds perfect, a song to tribute an ass kicking." We hit the bong one more time and call it a night.

Econome

The cost of living is starting to get out of hand. I can't help but wonder what the masses will do in the near future. I worked hard for my money and picking up my check these days is depressing. It's hard to get ahead, when the cost of living keeps going up, but the pay stays the same. The bosses have to know the economy is getting worse; they have to know some are not able to make it. I'm a single man so I don't have to worry about kids and a wife, but I get fucked on taxes. I have a few write offs and would make a decent living if I could keep the government out of my wallet. The thought of going through a depression in this day and age. Still no good news though.

On occasions I have made it in the rat races, but either blow it, or I abuse it. I have to have that greedy, soul less people; my sad job depends on them. My bills wait for their approval, a signed check. I stay to myself though in my shop. I work alone, which is fitting, but I do my job and get out. The last thing I want to be is a motionless target. I'm not sure where I'm going in this life, but I'm not even sure a person can get ahead like this.

So I'm stuck, a tax number. All working does for me anymore, is just get me by. Is this life? I hope not, that would be sad to miss out on so much. They tell me life is short. I wish the economy would let up on me, so maybe I can live a little more.

On the flip side

Spent my night in someone else's arms, my shattered mind not thinking quite right. I was on a train, early dawn, trying to find what life had for me. She said she didn't want to be with me, so I drank alone in the Amsterdam dark light. Feeling like a bum drinking in the morning hours, passing out on a park bench in front of a cathedral, wishing I had spent my night in someone else's arms.

I walk in the misty morning hours, trying to find who I am, what side do I belong to? What's right, what's wrong? What's wrong with me? What do I want to prove in this short life? The coffee shops were now open, deciding that sleep was not an option; I go in to make my mind up. The sweet aroma fills the air, only a couple of people, the way I like it. I smoke drinking coffee, talking to various people, prying almost. Was I the only one who didn't know?

I order a ticket back to the states I had to go figure out something, but until that flip happens, I have to work. I can't get out poor, yet I'm no greedy swine. I'm just caught in the middle of society. So I drank until passing out on the couch and decided I would try and figure it all out tomorrow when I was going to be forced to think for hours on the plane ride back. I didn't have a home to return to, spending too much time in Europe. I don't feel like I

was running from something, but rather
looking for something. It wasn't the fucking
a beautiful Dutch girl, or the endless
drugs, maybe it was the sky always being
grey?

"Give me a pint please sir. I leave for
the states tomorrow Ian." "A few on me eh.
I'll see you again though eh?" "Yeah you
know me by now Ian I'll be on the first
plane back out." We laughed knowing it was
probably going to be true. I go to the train
station and wait, regretting leaving
already. Having to leave all those habits
behind, to find what? I know I just needed
someone's familiar arms.

Hotel de Invalids

Forgetting me, but not the times, you were a walking body, still out of mind. We are all destined in some way, never understanding why? Never really living life anymore, not even taking the time to attempt anymore. This is just another winter gone; this year didn't seem to last as long. Just leave me a cigarette, along with a head full of guilt and regret.

We drank yesterday away, smoke most of today away, and was this wrong? Never satisfied, I could tell by that look in your eyes, the way you turn your hips and walk away so carelessly. Some was shame; some of the events could have changed, maybe changing future events. Our old friend boredom lurking in the back of our minds, disagreeing, always wrong. But this spring

didn't last too long, never
again, it's forever gone.
Sitting, smoking my last pack of
cigarettes, with my head full of
bad memories and even more
regret.

Never like you, not even from
a different time, just wanting
something else to pass my time.
Until my time is up, you'll
always look at me to blame, from
your way down from the clouds,
but when you come back; this is
where you'll stay. We will
reunite and live our days in the
house on the hill, this is where
I stay, this is my home.

I get carried away

I spent every last penny I could, but also saving to get out of here. The problem is I never get very far, if anything I always end up at the same place, same situation. I question myself to much about what I am doing in this place. I don't want to be alone, but see no other way out, any light at the end of this tunnel. "Mike why do you want to move there", is all I hear from people. I guess I believe in my mind that maybe I'll have better luck with a fresh start. Maybe the band will do better elsewhere. Maybe this little piggy has had too much wine. So I continue to sit here, alone, drinking my booze, smoking my smoke, this makes me happy and mad.

Something has to get me out of here, something needs to save me. Maybe the women and the scene that follows is what have driven me to my madness, this night time scene? My thoughts carry me away though. I think of how somebody may want to read my creations one day, the thought of enjoying my life and it's ingredients that make it mine. I get carried away at the thought of being happy with a woman, with a woman being happy with me. I want to have passionate love, not just a fuck and then darting for the door. I let these thoughts carry me away from reality for a while, it's pleasant. No money though to fund this unknown life that I want so badly. I could move to another random place, but it wouldn't feel like home either.

It's too easy to get carried away about the things that we don't have, what we think we want to posses. It's frustrating, but it keeps dreams alive to, kills the others. You get carried away when loneliness sets in.

I miss you, I guess I should

She left me again. "You know how
many fucking women I let talk to me
that way Jana? I normally don't put up
with this shit, these games." "That's
all I am a game to you, you don't want
to be with me." "You told me ten
minutes ago that it would be easier to
just change who I am."

"Fuck this and fuck you, you told
me on the way over here that you were
done with it all, so fuck you." I hung
up the phone, but it was never over
until she decided. Jana was growing
bitter towards me, yet her insecurity
held her back from what she wanted to
really say. Jana wanted me to do her
dirty work. "You always put me in a
hard spot. It's hard to want to be with
you when you bust my balls every other
day." "So this is how you want it?
You're really going to hang up on me
again, this is what you want?" "No," I
reply and hung up the phone. I didn't

want it to be that way; she wanted it to be like that.

I loved her as much as I could. If I would have loved her anymore I would have only caused her more pain in the end. There was going to be an end and we both knew this. It upset Jana and she refused to acknowledge it and I couldn't help but think about this sad day. Jana wanted that day to come sooner than planned. I wasn't what she wanted; I was a passing of the time. I could have played the role and broke her heart; at least this way she hates me instead.

I won't lie; maybe sometimes I don't want to go. After hearing Jana's remarks I don't want to be with her. This place has lost all its meaning, a distant thought of cheerful days that always seemed carefree, even though they never were. I miss all the good times. The times when we would stay up all night getting high, laughing, never answering the phone.

I can't forget the things she did to me to. Yet I miss her. I'm sick of this fucking plague I can't escape, what I can't give in.

So I see her at the gas station, at the bar, our favorite restaurant I hate and when I see him as well. You get to see what you were traded in for. It's like a used car lot, she probably traded up, but it's probably a lemon, that stupid bitch. I gave her music, laughter, passion and love, my love, fuck my love.

I leave her presence, I can't see her. "Hey Mike can you get me some pot?" "Hey Jana, no I can't get any pot. I could put in a call." "It's okay; I had heard that you moved." That's when I realized she called to talk. It's nice to hear her voice, but not worth it. I didn't want to think of him or her. I guess I still missed her. "Yes I'm moving to a place far away and I'm making my big move in a month." "Well good luck Mike, I mean that." "I'm sorry I couldn't help you with the weed, if anything changes I'll message you."

I had the weed, but did not want to see or hear her anymore, I missed her and she thought I didn't care. She makes me feel like it's raining outside. All of my friends that were girls all had boyfriends and had no time to numb me, fuck me. We all lost touch, due to them, the way they slipped through my fingers. "I feel like you're the only one who gets me, my soul." I've had a girl tell me and now Ash won't even return my call or messages. Had I become nothing? I guess I should miss them all; I don't blame them for not forgiving me. I wish they could believe me, if they would just miss me, but they were far in mind and body as I distant myself from a far away crowd. Who am I and who were you to miss. You fucked me over, you both did. I'm not a bad person, but I wish nothing good for you in the future.

I put myself in mourning

Life has become good to me. The checks come, the wine flows and the smoke smokes. I hate my job, but a man *has to have a job and I have bigger* plans for my one and only life. I finally get the music equipment I've always wanted, the women that every man wants, the time to travel and a little next egg. This is all very different and scary to me. I'm not use to this way of life, I feel like anything could happen at any time. It's not paranoia; it's just the simple fact.

I sit though and write. I write and I get depressed. This depression puts me in a mourning that fuels my writing and my music. If I didn't have the depression and mourning for life, then I would not be able to write. I would feel like I had no soul. It's not a matter of what I will do next; it's about needing to mourn on certain subjects and loves of life.

A lot of ways it is relieving to let these emotions flow through my

fingers in many forms and actions. I
can't make excuses, nor do I want to,
but the truth is I like the mood better
than acting like I like you, or certain
things about me. Life is too short for
some bullshit. The truth is, no matter
how many people talk to me, or think
they know me, I will never change. If I
changed then I wouldn't exist, like I
said I would be soulless. So I choose
to put myself in mourning. Don't ask me
why, don't care, just ignore me and my
ways. Let me mourn for my life.

My sunshine girl

She wakes, never to disturb me.

She goes to work as the sun begins to
shine.

I love her more every day; I love her
in the most complex simple way.

Scared to talk, not wanting to misguide
the passion.

Loving her, but mistakes made, but a
love for her I could never change,

so I turn off the radio, she's running
late, convincing her to stay.

So we lay naked for many hours,
talking, holding, fucking.

All this life together as the
sunshine's through the shades

My sunshine girl left

Never returning, I drove her away

She left me for another

Like so many love stories before

No matter what though, I will always
have my sunshine girl.

Time will pass and so will the memory

I can only hope so

I didn't want to
Waste the time

Boredom drives people to madness. Sometimes this can be good, sometimes even a fuel. It's now Thursday night and I decided now to write about last night. I didn't want to waste the time last night to write.

I took some mushrooms and decided to trip for some fun, a change of pace. I start out with a weird head change, almost made me sleepy. This stage passes quickly though, so I eat some more, not even being able to taste the nasty fungus at this point. The next stage for some reason is the best. I become productive during this stage. I couldn't see straight enough to write. Since I spend most of my day's writing, I decided that I wanted to get other projects done during this confusion. I sit in front of my record player and listen to all the greats that I haven't heard in a while. The phone rings and I'm hesitant to pick it up at first. I could use some reality to bring me back though. "Hey Mike what are you doing? Do you mind if I come over for a bit?" It was my friend Amy. "I don't know Amy; I'm in a weird state of mind, a wasted state of mind. I'm too fucked up, how about a rain check?" "Whatever Mike, you're just a fuck off, will you ever change?" I proceed on with my journey, not allowing the phone call to make my trip go bad. When a trip goes bad, that's when a man turns to madness. Hell I seen my cousins run naked into a field and wasn't found to the next morning.

I go to the recording room, around 2am

in the morning. I loop a guitar riff and crank it up. Then I jump on the drums and whale away. I ended up naked, passed out with a bottle of wine in my bedroom corner. I had to go to work. I just curled back up, drop the bottle and pretended it was Saturday morning instead. I decided to get up, eventually, and write about last night. I got high and wrote what I could remember. I thought about my mind set of not wanting to waste the time last night and it was basically because of a fungus, a fucking fungus. I start to think of all the time I wasted because of some sort of drug.

I let a lot of life slip through my thin fingers. Yes it is true that I have endless material to write about for the rest of my life, but I still could have lived more life. Being a fuck up is fun, but always take care of your shit. I'm a fuck up, I always will be, but I make the time now to do what needs to be done. If you are unable to make the time and you can't handle your shit, then fuck off you leaches.

If she only knew

If she only knew what she has done
to me?

The way she would look into my
eyes, covering up all those little
lies,

If she only knew how sweet she
smells, how sweet she taste,

She will never know, because I
will never tell her,

I love her, but she will never
know,

She will never know my reasoning
for loving her.

I will never really know why I
have come to love her.

Could it be her sexuality, the way
she comes out of the shower naked and
wet?

The snap of my fingers and she was
gone,

I drove her away, knowing, but not having a choice, always scared.

She told me I was scared of life, but I refused to listen, I refused myself the pleasure of her.

She will never know though.

I see her, I see her in the arms of other men and it kills me inside.

I love her, but I could never tell her this,

That would probably make her like me less, so she will never know.

So I live my little life, the life we could have shared, but I would never allow that, but I love her and she will never know that

Individuals

I am myself, like you somehow, living fast on borrowed time.

Always in a hurry, never going anywhere, the thought never even crossing our minds.

Cause I was myself, like you somehow, where did we go, did we ever leave? Did we listen, did we ever believe?

Because you are yourself, like me somehow.

I never understood, but then again I never asked why, never really cared, it's all been wasted time.

Maybe you love to rush to nowhere, but not me. I'm in a hurry to get somewhere.

Where though? Maybe from me. I am myself like you somehow...........

Junk Mail

"What the fuck is the shit in my mailbox? I come home after a week and this just randomly happens". I was yelling this to myself as I checked my mail after getting back from Europe. There was a note mixed in with my mail. It read, Mike elephants forever, and then had a little elephant drawn at the bottom. I start to freak out. I come in and open up a beer and look at the hand writing. I could tell it was a woman's and not a man's, plus it smelled of perfume, familiar perfume.

The kicker to all this was the fact that this had been an inside joke with an old flame. Nobody knew of that little picture of the elephant and how she writes. I didn't understand. I had told her a year before to never contact me again. She had married and that song had been played too many times. I had no idea how she had found me. I moved far enough away so we wouldn't run into each other. We had no mutual friends, nobody knows where I live. Yet somehow

she found me again, she always found
me. I guess I should have expected this
after a week and a half of mail piled
up, nothing but bills and fucking junk
mail.

The worst part was the old flame
had hand delivered another letter. The
letter was too long and started out
rough, so I disregarded it. I had been
receiving this type of mail for a few
months now every since I published my
last book. Nobody cares who you are
until they think you are somebody. I'm
still nobody, but some people have
caught wind of me, or caught wind that
I existed. I lived around certain
people for years before they even knew
I wrote. So I guess on the other hand
the junk mail was at least some
encouragement.

Bukowski would see ex coworkers
after quitting the post office and they
would ask what he had been up to and he
would tell them writing. His coworkers
never even knew. People tend to
acknowledge your existence when they
believe your something that you're not.
It's dumb, but true. It's basically
like the groupies of the band that suck
my dick just because I hold a guitar in
my hands and play in front of people

and get a few cheers. These are the people who don't have a love for anything. Just don't hand deliver junk mail to my house for me to come home to. I'm not interested in your opinions on what you translate my words to. I'm not even sure sometimes what I am writing about. Release me from your grief you inflict on me, accusing me of being someone that I am not.

Knees again

Ripping through,
Squeezing ever so slowly through my skin
I can taste the blood in my mouth
Even though it's just a mistaken identity
for life, to real to ignore.
It's crazy how one can misinterpret one
thing
For another
How one can feel the ripping of the skin,
But when I think I taste the blood and
don't, I worry,
I ask myself if it's really back,
Where is the signs telling me what is really
happening?
What's really going on?
Who knew this could bring me to my knees.
Makes me scream," WHY?"
Making me question the point, that exact
point in time, the reason for this torture
this pain.
This was not caused by you, which would make
you special.
This is caused by me, my own mind,
Which is worse than all of you?
Or maybe just because I know you?

Long road to a simple life

The years have come and the years have long been gone. Friends made, friends gone, now everyone standing next to me is only my enemy. What was said, what actions have been taken? We need our music; we need our medicine to comfort our souls. Did you ever believe me? The long road with no light, did you believe me?

Can I ask you to wake me up, maybe you know somebody who could, it should be easy, and we know who our enemies are. It's a bad dream, just walking in the dark, down a long road. Wake me up, shine a light, light a candle, show me something, and make me feel something. This long road took years to build, but only days to tear down, to sink. Show me something I've done, don't show me a mirror, and show me a picture. For something so simple it's taken me to a long narrow path.

Show me what I am sinking in. It's not my time to wonder why. The road still crumbles as we rely, no beautiful taste. This all could have been easier. If we had worked together or harder than maybe this road would have stayed strong as the days go by. We all missed the point as it falls all around me. It could have been easier just by you alone.

Never was

Lighting up a joint and drinking a beer, while sitting in the old jam room. It's sad to have so much passion for something and not being able to do it. It's like that first beautiful girl you noticed. I look at the drum set, amps, guitars, organ, mixer and many other things I've invested in. I look and it makes me sad.

Playing solo is like masturbating, yeah it gets the job done, but it's not the same. Playing with a band causes more energy to flow. I'm reminded of certain memories and arguments. It sucks having that passion along with faith, love, it leaves you open. Most people are lazy and selfish. I myself am just selfish. It sucks to think of what could have happened. What could have been? Most likely nothing, but maybe? I start to think of selling the equipment.

I think I'll start selling this shit tomorrow. Might as well get one more pick on the old guitar and one more bang on the drum. In the end my excuses are fucking useless. And that is why I am a NEVERWAS. Still the guitar is like an extension of my dick.

Not Enough

It's late, all alone
Nobody to talk to, everybody's home,
dreamless night again,
But that laughter in your eyes was just
crying in disguise,
I put you through pain, and I sit
thinking it's never enough,
Enough cigarettes and a head with every
thought consumed with regret.
It doesn't seem that there has been
enough time for all this madness in this
world created around us. You whispered, when
they said you shouted, when you did the
obvious to get out. To make this enough of
what they all need to let us go, let me go.
The guilt and regret still consuming my
thoughts on this sleepless night and when I
look out my window I see it is also a
starless night.
This reminds me of what so many people
did not get enough of. Enough money, love,
hate, attention, drink, power, pussy, or
maybe just bitterness. Whatever selfish act
that takes over our life and forcing us to
forget that there has been enough. I choose
to believe that we all will figure this out
someday, maybe soon? Through all this I know
I'm no better and that this is what it has
become. Not just any day, just the next day.
Not so much the present as it is the future.

?

Politics,

Religion,

Women,

Life,

Death,

Common sense,

Suicide,

Old,

Young,

New,

Original,

Love,

Hate,

Passion,

Driven............................

Shadow people

I kissed her goodbye, a fake kiss to keep her happy. "I love you Mike." "I love you to baby." This was a lie. I was not going to miss her and I didn't love her. Her name was Terra and she was gorgeous. She would bend over backwards for me and has.

I walk down the side walk as I see a shadow getting bigger, closer to me. "I just wanted to kiss you again." "Thank You." I walk alone down the streets of this great city that has become my new home. People questioned why I had to move so far away. "There are too many shadow people here." "What are shadow people," was what they would ask every time. "It's the same people," I would reply.

So I walk down what most people would call a lonely long road and I call it my life. Back at my old home, everybody and everything became the same. There was nothing different. Everything became the same. Maybe it was because we were all subject to the same visuals and audio. It's hard to tell when you are stuck in the middle of your life, surrounded by shadow people.

Nobody knows or cares for me in this city. I meet women like Terra and play that role of a semi-boyfriend for them. Some love me for it and some become hateful not understanding me, what I have become. I feel like this place is not cursed, but maybe I am still cursed for whatever reason. The women come and go, but this city is right. There are no shadow people, only individuals. Even though me and these people know each other, we still understand each other in that, leave me alone, mentality, fuck me physically.

She's late again

She calls me late,

It's always late.

I shake the drunkenness from her voice,

Trying to understand her,

Never understanding her actions though.

I never understand why she was mean?

Why she calls at all,

Maybe it's a passing

Through this boredom,

This chapter of life, her and my life.

She arrives, drunk, just like always

Disrespecting me every time.

I guess we'll have to keep this charade
up for now

It's hard not to pick those late night
phone calls up

I don't know where she's been, or where
she is going

I just know I'm her late night call for
whatever reasons

Snoring little fucker

I tell him to move, I tell him to get
on his side of the bed.

The bastard rolls his eyes at me,
closes them and starts to snore.

But I love his snoring ass. Eight years
of sharing a bed, and like a woman he
takes it over.

He snores with his eyes open, but I
love the little fucker

You're my boy Brewtus!

Summers came and passed

IT would be early in the morning, we would wake and meet. No school, no worries about grades, or homework, just the thought of freedom. "Hey Mike let's go down to the swimming hole," my friend Josh would say. There was a nearby pond we swam in. It was clean and we had a simple tire swing we hung from the overhanging tree of the pond.

The next summer seem to be less fun, but still innocent. We had to start to mow some local yards on the account of our fathers. We still met at the local swimming hole, swimming, laughing and never needing any drug of any sort, just life, the few times drugs were not needed or thought of. The summers became shorter and hotter. They took away our innocent summers and replaced them with jobs and sports training.

My friends and I started to experiment more of what life had to offer. I remember that first joint, the joint that filled my lungs, the first drag of so many. We started drinking, most of us taking to it right away.

"Come on Mike I got a twelve pack." We had to sneak off and drink, never thinking of the consequences, there had seemed to never be any. The only consequences seem to be from our fathers. I started to see summers turning into real life.

Then one day I woke up and somebody had transformed me into a young adult. I was living like a bum, even with working full time. The young beautiful girls coming and going like a revolving door. I was a nobody and the girls were faceless.

The summers were no more. They had only lasted a few years. A few years of no worries, of freedom. No debt collectors, no landlords, no whores, no addictions, just the addiction to life, gone. Everybody reading this will never get that back. From this point on we are in a sea of the human rat race, participants.

Summers now are the same as the winters, just the changing of the clothes.

The deluge of insolence, the aftermath

It sad when the mass is captivated by the idiot box. It's the way the world tells you what to do. This is a treatment that carries on for a few decades now. There is nothing we can do.

The people creating this mass brainwashing, speak against it, but continue to spew shit from their mouths and actions. I try to stay away, afraid it will hypnotize me like the people I see, I am human and could possibly be weak to its powers. Some people have to make it home at certain times to be sure and catch their program, as they call it.

People create ass grooves and drinking glass water rings that took years to get that groove just right. It becomes their chair, their routine. It's falling apart like our economy; there are too many ass grooves, too

much time taken, abused. The heat
scaring people. Taking care of the
places surrounding you is not heard of.
People just keep getting their daily
doses while never knowing it.

Only a few people will read this.
This much I know has become a fact, a
sad fact. I guess we will see what
happens next. What happens if some of
this is brought to their attention? At
least the mass would have a choice to
make and hopefully the ending will be a
little better wrote.

Tight lipped with a big mouth

She never tells me her name, yet I never ask it. I know her name is Jana though. I heard her on her cell phone tell someone, "Jana never flakes, you know me."

"What's the deal with you and that one girl," Hahs would ask in an almost natural cloud of confusion. On the other hand though it seems that everybody knows everything before me. "Mike I really like your book, I couldn't understand what chapter six was about…" and it enrages me.

I always stay quiet, scared that if I say anything that people will think they know me, or assume other things. I freeze up around people for good reasons.

I'm a nobody, but I do have some stalkers who seem to put too much thought behind my words. Some far out shit and the rest regular stalker shit, like blood on paper. I have never made any money off this cursed writing, but some people treat me as if I have accomplished the unthinkable. That was my problem, it was the thinkable, my mind, I'm cursed in my plague.

"Please leave Jana." "What a fucking surprise, maybe I should feel privileged, Mike knows my name." "Don't feel too special, I want you gone for good." I couldn't trust anybody, everybody thought they knew the real Mike, I was a nobody. People who really knew me just took advantage of me in ways that insulted my intelligence.

So I write, I write too much, revile too much, yet I'm sick of explaining to people the difference in real and made up ideas. Maybe I should not write and not be so tight lipped. You're not special enough to write about, you're made up. I don't care enough about the people in my life to give them the pleasure of thinking I would waste the time. The time it takes to think of a nightmare. I am Mike and you are nobody and I write about nobody. They are high times for me and wishes for you.

"Are you Mike? I and my girlfriend want to fuck you." "Yeah I know." "How did you know?" "You had to ask if I was Mike. It's obvious, that you both want to fuck me, just like the girl that left an hour ago. I'm sorry to disappoint you, but please leave me alone. We all know that there is no connection, no similarities, no passion, just a novelty. So I'll save you and me the afternoon so I can do what I do to keep young girls knocking on my door, so good day ladies."

To Many Times Said

Like the man on the television said, I had heard it all to. I can't get the evil out of my head, never forgetting, that would be too easy. Will this life be forgiven for all that I have become and done? Maybe tonight is the night I put the bottle down, yet against my will. It's just another day, like it's not suppose to be, but getting closer with every breath.

The breath that everybody dreads does not matter if they say they fear it or not, we all fear it. I feel as if this has been to many times said, or at least to many times thought? What we become in our personal success, becomes our forever know life. Why should we care, when we do every moment we are awake. I just hope that we still have the dreams in our sleep, a time meant for peace.

Too many times said, maybe not enough?

Unplug

I met this girl named Tiffany. She was
pretty, could probably do better than me,
fuck it, she could do better. Tiffany had
smooth dark skin, dark brown hair that was
like silk. She seems to always have that
fresh out the shower smell. We became more
than friends real quick. I would visit her a
couple of times a week. Sometimes going out,
or sometimes just staying in.

Tiffany started to ask me if I would
like to stay over. "Come on Mike, you won't
be sorry. Besides you're already here." I
had a hard time saying no. I layout on her
bed and she comes out of the bathroom in a
sexy outfit. Some teddy action. Tiffany
grabs the remote and turns the television
on. We both do our thing, me being very
unhappy with her performance. Lazy and
lifeless and then I had to hear her shitty
television shows in the background. I chop
it up to booze and weed, I figured with a
body like that, she deserved a second chance

Tiffany and I hung out quite a bit.
She was very passionate when we were out in
the clubs, the shows. She would kiss me
passionately. I would take her back and she
would always invite me to stay, "Mike your
already here." I would stay and we would do
our thing depending on how fucked up we both
were. Tiffany would always turn on her
television. She had a CD player that I would
offer to turn on instead, but she would say

it helps her sleep. I on the other hand
thought it was a distraction for the both of
us. It couldn't be healthy to have random
bullshit television, feeding you whatever
they want, especially while fucking.

I was beginning to worry about this
television problem. Tiffany was sexy and
passionate, but in her bed she was distant.
We had been to a show; Tiffany had hung on
to me the whole show and after asked if I
would stay with her. We get to her
apartment, that somehow smells good all the
time and she says she is going to change. I
quickly get up and try to find the right
cord to unplug the television. She has her
stereo and DVD player, but I find it. I
unplug only it. Tiffany comes out looking
like shit that I've dreamt about just about
wetting myself. She reaches for the remote
and tries to switch the television on. It
puzzled her and I told her the storm might
have shorted it out. I ask her if I can put
on a CD and she says, "I guess so, since the
TV won't work. I'm not sure if will be able
to sleep." "Well Tiff you look sexy, why
don't you worry about sleeping after while."
Tiffany's passion that I had seen other
places, started to come out, slowly at
first, then she was into it one hundred
percent. Clenching me, no distractions, no
car salesmen, and no bad early morning
commercials, just me. The next morning she
told me she hadn't slept that good in a long
time. I smiled and went in for some morning
time. Tiffany is passionate again. After we
were getting dressed and she had went to the
bathroom. I reached over to plug in the TV
and decide not to. It did her some good and
she did me good. TV sucks anyway.

What was her name?

Long haired brunette,

One blonde streak in the front.

It was cold out and to draft in my
room, I was alone, who to call?

I seen her walking into the bar, the
dive that I sat at every day, right
down the road.

Her legs were gorgeous, they seemed to
keep going, and she looked like she was
walking in slow motion, knowing I was
looking at her.

I see her face, such beauty, so natural
yet sad behind the eyes.

My blood was still pumping, maybe too
fast, yet still alone, too far from my
home.

Later going to her asking her name, but
I only remember our shame.

I remembered her beautiful face in
great detail and her beautiful blonde
hair.

Sure I didn't know her name and she
didn't know mine, but I can't help
wondering sometimes what happened to
what's her name

Us

Sorry for being me. Sorry for never
setting you free.

Our friendship meant so much to me,
even when you would get mad and leave,
leaving a lonely soul.

A lonely soul I'll always be, nobody to
understand nobody for me, for my
simplicity.

Feelings changing with the cold season,
letters telling what needs to be told,
meanwhile I didn't know.

Stupidity, selfishness, the book about
me, what other explanation could there
be.

We lost our path, we never saw the
life, the opportunity, Jesus gave up on
me long ago, but we lost our path.

Wise man is not an offered path to me,
or the note would have never been
given, maybe never even wrote.

She hurt me once and walked away

Why did I lie?

It's early and the sun isn't up
yet, just peace and quiet. I wait for
the coffee to finish before I light my
first cigarette for the long day ahead.
I turn on some tampon rock to not break
my morning dismembered mind from lack
of sleep. I like to smoke a joint while
in this morning haze, getting me higher
than any other time I smoke, the only
time I can get this relaxed.

The coffee is done and I take a
cup outside and turn the CD player up.
I smoke a joint and feel the best I
know I'll feel that day. I have to be
alone with myself today. Everybody is
out living life, going to work, or they
hate me for good reasoning. Life is
punishing me. I can't forget the sound
of her voice. I loved her very much, so
I knew that this morning was the only
time that I would care less than later,
being reminded by everything.

I knew her to long and she never came close to knowing me. The poor woman was kind, devoted and put up with me too long. Sure she was insecure who displayed this emotion too much, which ultimately was our down fall and me. I couldn't be a man and set her free. Yes I was leaving and would never return to hear her name, but at times I wanted to ask her to go with me, to never return. To try what everyone else was scared to try. Today was about making it through without slipping, without letting me in.

I feel like if it was raining outside it would fit with the way I felt. I sat outside, stoned, on my third cup of coffee and already I was thinking about her, about my lie. She lied to, many, many times and now I was about to be on an eleven hour plane trip away, thinking of her. "I invested too much time into you Mike. I can't believe what you've done to me, how sad I am, sad on my outlook on life because of you, I hope you can live in your misery, the misery you claim to love because it is unstoppable you say." I did say all that and I did behave in the manner she spoke of. It tore me up though knowing what she thinks of me as a person. A person who was once in the same spot that many other's has long filled before me. I should be over it, but that is something easier said than done. The passion and companionship was gone, gone forever. I was an eleven hour flight away for many reasons. I was going to end up a flight away, for reasons that were set before meeting her, before holding her soft skin. I really did think about having her with me right now, but now I was to not hear about or from her. Her life without me, to accidentally see her at the gas station and see her smile, a smile contributed by someone else. No more, I made sure of that.

Beautiful women surround me and all I can do is think about a woman back in the states. I binge too much to stop the pain I have created. Cheap women, booze and fake friends was my life now. If I would have asked her, she would have said yes and I would be enjoying this place more to share and not be alone for once in my life. Like many though, I do not hold the power to predict the future or change the past.

So now I keep living my passions with one piece missing and accept that we will never be. I'll never see her when we come through our home town to play. The tour is over right now though and I survived it, trying to conquer more all the time. Right now though I sit on my terrace and wish I would have asked her, but I never had to lie again, I could have been a man. That's something I question myself to many times. It's going to be a long lonely day.

You're just somebody I use to know

Thinking back on that terrible sad day, I feel like the biggest asshole. Teasha and I were neighbors and we were at that age of curiosity. I remember how cute Teasha was, but not all of the guys at school thought so. I believe it's because she was like me and wasn't in that pack of girls who have everything. Kids can be so shallow. I was shallow, our day's or evenings of hanging out were great, and she was interesting. I was shallow for one reason. Teasha had grown to like me and I could feel it, but did not feel the same way back, not like that, not yet. I was dreading the day after school when she would spring this on me.

The afternoon came and I told her I couldn't. I don't know why, I had never cared what people thought so I don't think it was that, I'm certain it wasn't that, but I'm not certain what it was though.

We remained great friends, still experimenting even though we were just friends. I looked forward to weekends when our parents would let us stay out all night. I believe our parents still believed we were too young to be experimenting, but we were past those innocent years, but not all of them, not all of our innocent years, not yet.

Teasha left one weekend to go stay with her real mother. I was sad. Those years you're trapped to your neighborhood, so I would be sad one weekend a month due to her absence. This particular weekend though was different. Teasha had tried to cross the street and was hit by a car while at her mothers. She was so young. I heard my mother talking about somebody that just died, but she was being quite. My mother told me what happened, the whole story. I went to my room crying wondering why. Teasha would never get to go to a prom, get a driver's license, make love, live life. It made me angry and sad; I was cursed with pain, my sinking heart. I wish at the time that death would bring me my last breath.

Teasha and I would never ride our bikes together again; we would never

lie on the roof kissing, talking. I
didn't understand death at the time,
not knowing how to feel, what to think.
They buried Teasha three days later.
The funeral was big, and now that I'm
older I am real familiar to familiar
with death and the power it posses, but
the funeral was the first of too many
for me to attend. My mother and I sat
in the overflow room and then we did
something that I had no idea what took
place at some funerals; we were walking
up to view the body. My mother told me
it would be good for me to view the
body. At the time I didn't understand
why. I remember every detail while
walking down that dark, long walk way
to the front in that old church, where
chairs squeaked and people sitting
shoulder to shoulder in their best
clothes. It was quiet and my mother
held my hand as we made our journey to
the casket that seemed so far away.

My mother leans over to look at
her and I see a tear roll down her
cheek and I become scared, I try to
hold back my tears when stepping up to
see Teasha for the last time forever.
I stepped up and she looked so
peaceful, that was the first time I
felt death. I wanted to lean forward

and tell her that I loved her. Tears roll down as my mother grabs my hand and pulls me away from Teasha forever. There were too many people there that would never know her the way I knew Teasha, at least not what we created.

I tried not to ask why, but couldn't help but wonder. This is the first time I had my encounter with depression. I would lie down at night, trying to sleep, but instead stifling my sobs in the late night hours. I would ride my bike to all of our little hideouts. We both lived next to the train tracks and had a hideout between our houses that was a cement hideout under the tracks. One day after leaving there I rode my bike by Teasha's house and her father was outside and was on his mower crying. I stopped and asked Robert if was okay as I looked at his yard that was mowed in spots. Robert told me he mowed her name in the lawn, he thought maybe she could look down and see it. He cried and I was sad for him, if it were that simple I would send her a message. Being a kid I had no idea how to handle my role in this situation. Finally Robert said he had to put the mower up and I was relieved. I went home and when I went to sleep

that night listening to Bob Dylan's,
knocking on heaven's door, remembering
our times together. This was the first
time I had learned about death, but not
the last.

A-dam

I look out my old window that
lifts up, no screens, just an old
window. All I see is cobblestone
streets and tall skinny homes. The
chilly air coming through the window
filling my small room with the smell of
the streets. I haven't chosen this life
of loneliness, but I live it because
it's all I know.

There are yells and distress calls
all through the air, but still cold and
alone, asking myself, where is my body,
where's my mind? What is it that makes
me insane, what is it that takes up my
time? Why can I not go back?

Was it the art, the surrounding
beauty, the shame this city has to
offer to a lonely man like myself, all
so captivating? I never was able to
allow myself to be free, or free
myself? I'm off balance and still
alone, but I feel as though I try.

I try to pick up the phone and dial an unknown name as I begin to see the streets fill with many types of people, going somewhere, going nowhere? As the streets fill, I slip into an unknown loneliness, but I never make that unknown call. Wherever and whoever she is, she is back home sleeping and I'm alone.

But I am on this journey to find that, "maybe," the hope we all crave, a place to call home.

A day to buy back

"Come by Mike, my parents are gone and my aunt is gone." What if somebody comes back?" "So?" That was enough reasoning for me. I remember that day with such detail and in happiness. We were so young and our bodies were changing. I felt great being around Allison and now was my chance to be alone. Being as young as we were, neither one of us had explored the opposite sex's bodies yet. It felt slow and it made me anxious.

Allison put her hand into mine and I felt tense, but good. We had lain down on her bed, holding hands enjoying silence and conversation. Allison curled in my arm which had made it around her somehow and I felt nothing but that moment. I held her in silence, feeling how fragile she was. The smell of her skin will forever haunt me. Wonder where she is now?

The night falls too soon, but I
stay and we go outside. We jump on her
roof finding a ladder in her garage.
We hold hands again as we laid down.
Allison leaned over and kissed me. I
had never made out with a girl, but
it's a natural action and exhilarating.
I know that I never wanted it to end
and now years later I understand why.
That was the best turning point in my
life. The natural rush of the
unknowing. Sometimes I wish I could
find a roof to jump up on and sit up
there with a girl and have that feeling
once again. Feelings like it could be
wrong but isn't. The day meant so much
to grow as an individual, as a person
period. Sometimes in a pathetic way I
think back to that night and smile.
Sometimes I wish you could buy back a
piece of the past, lost time.

Now though, we have all become
familiar with death, hate, love,
stature and how people are capable of
being. Allison grew and knew what I
would become, like many other women who
did experience this, the experience of
me. But that town doesn't exist
anymore. It was fucked in its plague
and so was our innocents. We all moved
to fucking fast, rushed into life. Now

I know we felt so much more, I know it
meant so much more, but life goes on
with or without our sorrows.

Airwaves

Could it have been spoken a little
louder, what were you asking for? You hear
it on the airwaves, you just didn't quite
get it, but you still got out somehow. This
self created hell you choose to call my life
in attempting to assassinate me. It doesn't
mean anything at all though; you just do as
you're told by these cowards that control
our airwaves.

Maybe you couldn't think on your own?
Say what you want to say, you shouldn't just
repeat what you're told. I myself choose to
stay away from those fat fingers telling the
world what to do. Were the airwaves ever
pure? Have they every served the masses in a
respectable sense, not assuming they are
idiots. That's what they become though, just
to keep up with the cool kids.

I hear my grandfather talk about the
days of AM radio. He is also slipping into
senility. Who knew they would say that
though. People are getting their information
from the wrong sources; the people who
pollute the airwaves are just doing what
they are told just like all the other
robots, saying what they are told to say. I
will hide in those places nobody dares to
go, dreaming to escape, but everything being
more than I could try. It's a beautiful day
though, the sky is clear, maybe the airwaves
are being taking back, causing less

pollution, less chaos.

Buying a Persona

What does a person do when they don't like who they are? When they are so desperate to be like you, what does a person do? A world full of dilettantes, madness, and unoriginal robots was what I had to face every day. Impossible to defeat? Never, but none the less this was difficult, watching a friend buying his lifestyle. This made me sick, were we going to be taken over by dilettantes, were we going to have to debase ourselves because they had the money? I'll drink this cheap wine, think about this with every cigarette; spend too much time worrying about nonsense and things that shouldn't matter to me.

I will not let this deluge of dilettantes happen. Undeserving, young arrogant asshole's trying to fuck me out of my time. So I decided to do what had to be done, to take down the ones around me before they come after me. I smile and shake their hands. I do their jobs that are beneath them and take their money. I listen closely and fuck them right before they fuck me. This was the ongoing battle, while I see that young asshole's still are buying their persona, still pretending that they are actually something that they aren't.

I may think that I have something to do with nothing to learn, but I am wrong. I have to learn how to take these sheepeople down.

Dark Decent

It would be a hot Texas summer morning. Brian and Ray lived down the road from me and we would hang out just about every day. The days seemed longer back then, but not long enough when we were young. The heat never seemed to bother us; at least it didn't bother us until we grew older. I remember summer coming and being so excited, and then it was over as quick as a blink. We were innocent though and people let us be kids.

"Come on mike let's go to the pond, or go see Tammy in her pool". Tammy was slightly older and loved to tease us. "You want to see me naked Mike?" "Fuck yeah", I would reply excited. We would lie in her bed and explore each other's bodies, until her parents would come home. When it was time for me to come home, my father would stand on the front porch and whistle. I could always hear him whistle, it was loud and spanned out to every place that I would be at. It was just a simple time in those old Texas summers.

The summer's started to seem shorter every passing year. Suddenly we had lost our innocents, and no longer went to the swimming hole. We all had come from poor families, so we all mowed lawns and I helped my father in the oilfields and life had already seemed boring.

Then all of a sudden it was, "Get your ass up if you want to eat today". This is what my summers had turned to. Fun at the lake, or the thrill of just being out of the

house was long gone. The summers became
warmer each passing year, and nobody knew
it, but we all woke up one morning and we
were all a part of the world. What could we
have done though?

That was our decent into darkness.   I
lie in bed and smoke a cigarette now the age
of twenty six and wonder if or what
everything went wrong. Is this really what
life is, or will become? I just live day to
day after being told to do what I had to do
to keep from returning to my dark decent. At
the age of twenty six this was a hard task
to escape the hatred I have become full of.
If we could only go back to that old
swimming hole. If only we can go back to
exploring the unknown, the curiosity that
was buried deep within all our souls.

IF YOU'RE GOING TO TALK SHIT, THEN SAY IT OUTLOUD

Another gray, hazy, beautiful morning. I go downstairs and fill the air with the aroma of fresh coffee and weed. I drink a couple cups of coffee and finish up my smoke, and then I make my way upstairs. Jana is still asleep in my bedroom. She still looks gorgeous as she sleeps. I grab my notebook and pen and go back downstairs. I write for about two hours. I write about her, me, life as I perceive it. I feel like the writings are good and the coffee is better. "Mike what are you doing? Are you still writing from last night, you didn't even fuck me." "Well I'm sorry, but when you get in the zone, you don't want to leave."

I hear Jana mumble something as she turns around and walks away from me. I change to Irish coffee. Jana is complaining while she gathers her things. It's funny because when people want to they can gather their shit and go. Jana was taking too long, she wanted attention and the poor girl just couldn't get it from me. Jana fell too hard to quick for nothing. Jana should have never met me, but she did. Jana knows everything that I do, the way I live. Over time this doesn't matter though. Some women and men are this way and some are not. I see it as insecurity, not really a love. True love lies within truth.

So here I sit a small table, ashes everywhere and the next cigarette in hand. I wish Jana would hurry up and leave. I hear her mumble and sometimes shout unclear sentences. The sad thing is this is just one of many times.

I was an asshole and I admitted this to Jana to many times over. Jana didn't want to believe this and Jana never wanted to be wrong. Maybe it was my honesty that got me, maybe my lies? Jana never lied to me. She chose silence and denial to our downward spiral of childish arguments. Jana started to spy on me, telling me things that I didn't even know about me. I felt something smack the shit out of me from behind. Jana had grabbed a plate and hit me with it. The one time it wasn't a paper plate. I feel blood and

laughed. I figured it would have been a
knife to the back like before. I get
up, feeling like I have just been hit
by a plate, obviously literally and
asked her to leave. As the room spins,
I try to pull myself together, but I
yell. I yell to Jana about all the
sleeping around she done, the lies.
"When I have shit to say Jana, I say it
out loud, go the fuck away." I hated it
because it will never fade as long as
one of us goes on living. That's the
harsh reality of life. The great thing
was that I at least had her out of
sight. Now my plates are used for
eating and not for teaching me lessons.

Don't you see?

One my way to my dark decent, I wish there was a way to repent.

I'm not sure why, maybe the things people don't know about me, what I don't know about you.

I can't help but think of you in my last hour. You didn't push me here, I pushed me here, and you had no idea. Needing more, but needing isolation, so depression fills the void the huge hole in my lump of coal.

So hate me but never again, this is the time, this is the living end.

I'll take this one lifetime, I don't think that's a bad thought, just self pity, selfishness, tired, but not important.

Drunk as a poet

On pay day

My favorite day of the month. I have
finally started to generate some money
from my writings. Not much to brag
about, but enough to get excited about
when you are use to being broke. People
say, "Mike you'll have to give me a
copy of your book", but the people I
give a copy to never read it and it
cost me money, I just don't get them
free. I'm okay with this though, this
way nobody I know can convince
themselves that they know me. Never the
less though I have had some success in
the underground scene and sold a
collection of short stories and that
brings us to date.

    I bring my little check into the
bank to cash it. I cash it all never
saving any of it. I consider writing to
be a passionate hobby so I treated the
checks like one. I head to the liquor
store, money in hand, a smile on my
face. This is the only time of the
month that I get to buy imported beer,
a good bottle of vodka and a good

bottle of wine. I always go home after and start to drink. It's really the only time of the month that I drink with a smile on my face. I always drink and write alone for a few hours until usually around 12AM and then call up a girl. I like to drink with a woman afterwards when I don't want to think anymore about the future of my writings. Will I sell more and be able to live like this every week?

I wrap everything up and have the women out the door by 7Am and then I drink and write about the dumb opinions that these uninteresting woman spew. I do this until I find myself naked on the floor with empty bottles rattling as I struggle to get off the wooden floor, smiling the whole time. I light a joint, open the last beer, drinking it slowly, then I think about being a writer.

Flowers and Backdrops

Simplicity did always catch your eyes
Everything you talked about, but never
attempted to even try,
The important thing is the obvious thing
that nobody chooses to say,
You heard a true story told by this liar,
you tried but couldn't get any higher.
        Cause I lost my car downtown again,
lost while drinking with a unknown friend,
but everyone always falls down laughing, so
we decide to join them,
It seemed that their feet were moving so
fast with scenery arrangement changes, only
to confuse. I look for my bag that I want to
keep me today, could make me lazy along my
way, but when he felt worse he always did
his best, always putting normal to the test.
        Everybody just seemed to be flowers and
backdrops sitting in the right place at the
right time, what would they do next?

Hidden message

"Mike I want to love you but you
hate yourself so much that it is
impossible to attempt to even try."
She was right I did hate myself. I'm
sorry and wish she could forgive me and
leave me if she could. We had some good
times, but only when we were fucking.
I wish she would believe me if she
could. She didn't know that I had grown
to love our fucked up relationship.

Insecurity will drive a woman mad.
A man cannot live when his every move
is monitored and you only get one turn.
I wish she didn't care what I did and
didn't do. I write about her though.
She doesn't know I don't even know if
she has ever even read any of my
writings, my soul. She had me in the
palm of her hand, but she didn't know
this. "Mike I wish you would talk to me
let me in." "I don't know how to talk."
"You can sure as fuck write, but you're
quite and alone." I always had a hidden

message when I wrote about her and
there was always a hidden message about
a boy who loved a girl if she would
only read, but I fear reading is no
longer important to the masses. The
idiot box can tell you right away what
you want to hear and what, "they," want
you to know. The beauty of reading is
the independent thought, the passion,
the hate, the muse that inspired so
many. Inspired people so much that they
wrote about their life, the up's and
down's. There are many hidden messages,
but writers also wear their heart on
their sleeves leaving their selves
open.

I could never tell her or anybody
else what I think of them, but somehow
it's okay for them to tell me what they
think of me. This somehow sets fine
with me.

House of whores

Mexico can be a great place, it can also make you see the bad side if you look too hard, or too much. Everywhere I go in this world, I like to walk around late throughout the city. I was going to be in Cozumel for a couple of weeks clearing my head of life. It was always easy to jump on a plane and be in Cozumel in a couple of hours. I had been there many times and have walked it many times, late drunk, hanging with the locals.

I get up early the second morning I was there and walked down the road for a pack of cigarettes. The great thing about Mexico is you can get a drink anytime, anywhere. I grab a beer with my smokes and go sit on the ocean side as the cruise ships were off in a distance, making their way to the pier. I sat there and drank a couple more beers and decide to walk the city during the day. It was Monday and it seemed to have everybody going at a slow pace. I had seen this beautiful cathedral many times before that I walked up to. I decided I wanted a picture, so I went back to my room to get my camera. By this time it is noon at the island and it is more active. I go by the cathedral, taking pictures, admiring its natural beauty.

A man asked me if I would like to buy some. I get offered weed in every place I go, I guess they see the pothead within. I told the man I had enough but thank you. He said he was talking about pussy. The man was standing in the door way of the cathedral; you could see candles lit and a lot of girls praying.

"You like pictures friend? Come in and take some inside for five dollars". I go in and see a big Mexican man in the corner a sleep and even more girls. I asked the man why so many girls were praying and crying. He pointed up stairs and told me sixty dollars and I can fuck my choice any age. I tell the man no thanks, knowing not to start a scene, or to tell the man he is a piece of shit. I get up and see a young, beautiful Mexican girl holding a candle in the corner crying. The first thing that comes to mind is the song, "Whorehouse of screams". I feel bad for this girl, but I can't help her. I head out the door and the man stops me and ask if I'd found one I liked. I told him I had, and I had the money, but wanted to ask him about extras, but was shy and wanted to talk to him outside to smoke first, not feeling like smoking in a cathedral.

The pimp walks through and I flatten him out and quickly cover his mouth, looking at him with my finger over my mouth. The pimp shakes his head, so I keep my knee in his chest but uncover his mouth. I ask him what the fuck he was doing with these underage girls. The pimp said something in Spanish kind of loud, so I pick him up and drag him around the corner, covering his mouth again. "I said no yelling for help and speak clear English fuck head". He said he owned them. I asked him what made these innocent girls his to pimp? "The young one is my daughter you fucker, but I'll give you a discount". I stare at him and then on the ground there was an empty bottle. I grab the bottle and the pimp stands up to run. I hit him over the head and turned him over, spit on him and walked through the allies. I hit a bar, feeling bad for the innocent, they don't even know a little bit of normal.

I knew I would have to seek quick refugee before his goons saw or heard him. I stuck out though having tattoos all over to my hands. I get in a jeep that tourists left the keys in while at the gift shop, so I borrow one. I drop it off in the jungle about a mile from my hotel. Fuck that shit. I got away and the thought scarred me and what those poor girls had to mentally endure.

I need a phone call

I need a phone call, but who will
pick up and say, "Mike"? Would there
ever be someone to pickup? I decided to
go down the street to a little dive. I
arrive at the bar and the place reeks
of pitiful people and shameless acts
and thoughts. I just sat over at the
end of the bar, listening, but wanting
to ignore. The little dive had some old
sad country song playing over the
loudspeakers. It seemed fitting.

A woman walks in, looks around and
sits next to me at the end of the near
me. She was an attractive woman with
dark hair, tall slender body and
gorgeous eyes, my weakness. "Hello, I'm
Mike". "Hello Mike, my name is Jana,
how are you doing this afternoon Mike"?
"Not too bad, just having a beer, but I
have to ask the most common questions
asked in this place, what is a woman
like you doing is this dump"? "I moved

a few blocks away and needed a drink after a day of moving in. What are you doing Mike, sitting in a dark corner of a dive on a Saturday evening alone"? "I was thinking too much and decided to walk down here and get a drink. I also live done the road from this place, it's a dive, but close". Jana asked me if I minded her talking to me. She said she had been alone for too long and told me it was nice to laugh.

Jana asked me what I did for a living and I told her the truth, which was I didn't know what I really done in life. "Well how are you paying for my drinks and yours then Mike?" "Luck I guess", was what I told her. Jana told me that I looked like I could be a pothead. She asked if I had any after a couple of hours of talking. I told her no and told her I need to make a phone call. I go to the backdoor and slide out behind the boxes covering her view. She started to bore me.

It wasn't the poor woman's fault. No I had a previous woman who was my muse, set the bar to high for these bar flies to reach. I had grown pass the age of groupies. I needed that phone call to someone specially, a love, an eternal flame. One day I will call and

she will pickup and comfort me and
bring me back to what is known as
reality. I have long lost touch with
reality, people looking at me almost
curious. So I go back to my room and
open my address book and try to look
for someone to call and come up empty.
This drove me to loneliness, my best
friend. Meddling into life and true
friendship. I haven't spoke to her in
months. Why would she cut me out of her
life? I just moved, I didn't die. At
least not yet.

I thought I sounded sweet

Hearing the words that heather had told me, playing over and over in my head. I have never really had a way with words. It's just a gift that I don't posses. So I wrote her a letter. Heather thought it was a chicken shit way for me to communicate, but that was and is the brutal truth. I had told heather it was good living with her, but that was not the right thing to say to a lover moving out. I had become a frozen man. A pain in Heathers ass. "You are you're worst enemy." Is what I would always hear from her, she couldn't accept the fact that I knew this; I had informed her of this. I had thought I was kind at times though.

I couldn't dispute what her argument was. I had my moments, but my memory serves me right. I remember. Just because she didn't want to accept reality, I wanted to. I'm tired of ignoring everything. I thought I had told her in a sweet way. Heather knew her memory would always haunt me. No matter what she had control over my mind, but I could at least try. It wasn't right and it never would be, but this is just one fucked up situation.

Sorry I just received two more angry calls. I'm going to stop now. See you in a few years, but I'll talk to you soon...............

I don't want to see
The day it's dying

       There are many fears, to many that all of us have. Even the people who seem to have it together, they even have fears. A person with money might fear losing it all, or maybe a skinny person might fear of getting fat. I'm not sure, but I believe that everybody has some sort of fear.

       My fear is what I see happening in front of me every day. People have no common respect, even Texans these day's always seem to be pissed off. The way that people are, becoming emotionless towards other people. I hope I never turned this way, this bitterness, it was a scary thought. That was my fear.

       I guess there is a lot of life that I see dying. I'm watching the world not care anymore and I hope I am not a passionless person; I like to think I wasn't. Who knows though? I didn't want to see the day it was dying, but I believe a little more dies every day. I August 24th 1981, the music hushed and the wind died. I haven't seen the fear go away, or if the fear is even there?

The notes she wrote

I remember, I remember because I have
the evidence. The evidence proves to me
that Naomi and I use to exist. Naomi's
mother did not approve of me. Naomi
could have done so much more, but I was
dead weight for her. Naomi was the type
girl that had scholarships and I was
the kid popping little white pills. I
spent most of my time in the library.
I would read and write, trying to act
like I knew something about life. Life
seemed so much brighter then, of course
we weren't living in the real world
yet. I wish I could go back to those
days. I would sit in the library and
write Naomi.

I was so excited when writing her
letters. Naomi and I would exchange
letters in person, or we would mail
them to each other since we lived in
different counties. I loved the
simplicity of those days. I miss
waiting on the letters, waiting on her

thoughts about me and life. Naomi talked of beautiful things and kept me intrigued with her outlook, intrigued with the notes she wrote. I wish I would check the mail one day and find one of her letters. I doubt it though.

To much time had passed and we both had separate lives. We would have a lot to tell her and her to me, but would it be appropriate. Naomi would contact me and I would always try to initiate something, but I never felt right doing that. Sure I was a man now, no kid, built myself a brag able life actually.

That's why I go to Naomi's birthday party after all these years when she invites me, to see her face. I show up and her family is happy to see me, but shocked. I go through the routine of hugging everybody, but want Naomi alone. I finally got that opportunity and I took it.

Naomi and I took the chance to fine serenity in a darkness created by the building. I told her everything I should have told her years ago, but now it was too many years passed. I told Naomi, as we lay looking up. We could never go back to that simplicity. The good thing for me was being able to tell her of the crystal clear memory I had about our past and the notes I still had, but not living in any past, just a distant memory to dig up in a once of while.

Naomi and I start to tell our goodbyes as I start my truck. "Thank you so much for coming and I love you Mike." "I love you to Naomi." I got in my truck not wanting to leave. That last hug got me. Naomi's softness, her perfume, her natural smell. I think I died a little.

I need a way out

I want a way out,
I need new shoes,
Going to find a home, wherever that may be.
Cause I need a way out,
Could use a jacket
Such a cool breeze, brought myself to my
knees,
Needing a way out

It was always too much too fast,
Too little too late,
Four thousand seven hundred miles from what
I know,
I need a place to call home,
Because I'm on a train ride, all the phone
calls never made,
To scared to be with you,
Alone again and questioning all that is
going on,
Looking for a home, that's honest and true.
I need a way out,
Give me a way out, I couldn't find a way
out, so everybody could find a way out, so
everybody could find a way out from misery.

I chose to continue with my slow suicide
method, it's comfortable and practical

Just because you love Jesus
They think you're crazy

I was sitting in the county hospital ER waiting room. I had been ran off the road and left for dead by the asshole that hit me. My truck was finished, its life cut short. Of course it's Saturday night and all the crazies, junkies, homeless, the whole fun bundle was out and about. "I need a shot, something", one frail sad looking man yells. "I KNOW IT'S ALL IN MY MIND", another homeless man yells as he picks at his arms at a fast pace.

A woman comes through the door in a wheelchair; she's half naked saying she is closer to seeing Jesus. I start to feel better, but for some reason I get caught up in the ER sad drama of these people's lives. "She's always on my mind and nobody made us wait, but now I can't see anything, I just need to be caught when I'm falling", the woman to my right says. A man, who had been waiting for hours, finally got called to the back. I had heard him talking about needing some medical attention. I tell the nurse to take me off the list. I had insurance, so they would get me in quicker and these people were the one's needing attention.

The man keeps saying that they told him it was only in his head. "It's only in my head? It's only in my head? It's only in my head?" That's what he kept trying to tell himself. Meanwhile a nurse opens a door to the terrible smelling waiting room, letting in a shot of fresh air. The nurse finds the family of the old man who had been complaining about his chest for hours and told them he had passed away.

I know this is the job of the hospital staff and it probably becomes emotionless to them, but it was the coldest way to tell a person that their loved one is no longer with them. I felt bad for the family. Chaos was all around us and their loved one just blended in, in the eyes of the doctors. It was sad to see such disorganization. People keep coming and going, mostly junkies and homeless. I was listening to a girl cry from being beaten, I had to go get a strong drink, and my problems were mild compared to these people that seem to be in a different world anyway. A world I think I might know of?

"It's all in my head? It's all in my head"? I ask the man what was in his head. He tells me some crazy stuff that made me laugh in a bad way inside. He stands up and yells, "JUST BECAUSE YOU LOVE JESUS, THEY THINK YOUR CRAZY". The man leaves and I follow behind him. I think hard about what he said as I start walking towards my house. Feeling blessed and sad as I go into a bar. Many lives believed in Jesus. They go to a church and talk in tongues, run up and down the aisle, cast out demons and these people were not called crazy. These people who did nothing but talk about Jesus, they were called crazy. I wonder who is crazy.

All of this brings up interesting questions. The man in the ER said a lot in a little. He truly believed in his higher power and people really did believe that he was off his rocker. I decided to skip the bar. My head was killing me and it felt drained. I was fairly sure that I wasn't crazy, but what about the old man. What kind of eyes was he looking through and how was he looking through those eyes, what angle?

Life now

It feels great, but I also feel
like a jackass. All the prison issued
me was old khakis and a purple shirt.
I didn't care though it had been to
long since I have seen nothing.
Everything that happens in there, the
things that are unspeakable, they stay
at the prison cell, never to be talked
about outside of those walls. In
certain since, I was a new person.

Huntsville gave me shitty clothes
and a bus ticket, a golden ticket. I
was headed to Dallas, but had no idea
where I was going, what I was going to
do. I grab a pack of smokes, from the
money I had, that was legitimate in my
old bank account before the incident.
At one time I had lots of money, but
not now, just a nobody again.

I shot a man over passion, over
stupidity. I loved Tiffany and could
not stand the thought of her fucking
somebody else, even now. I lit a fresh
cigarette, the first one in six years
that wasn't stale as shit. I got out on

good behavior on parole earning a little time cut off of my sentence. I belonged to the state for another ten years of parole. The cigarette was great. The bus had another hour and a half until its arrival. I see a little bar, dive, and walk down to it. I feel like an idiot wearing those old mismatched clothes, but wanted to feel the burn of whiskey slowly flowing down my throat.

I walk in and the place is dark and sad, even for a guy fresh out of prison. I order two doubles. "You fresh out?" Most men getting out of prison like to wet there whistle here when they get out, even against their parole requirements." "Yeah six years." "I'm not one to judge, just to serve men their drinks. Any idea where you're going? Most men sit in here not knowing where to go, what to do." "I guess I'll go back to Dallas and beg for a job, it's the same as prison, except for the real pussy. I hear my bus pull up and run out to catch it.

Six years and nobody wrote, nobody visited, and they just assumed I was a cold blooded killer, but I was not. Tiffany was faithful, lovable, and passionate and she was mine forever. I loved her more than anything in this god forsaken world. Life wasn't worth living, so I was in my own prison either way. It wasn't Tiffany's fault; she was just sleeping, possibly dreaming, maybe dreaming of me. I was gone out drinking after a rehearsal. I was feeling lonely for some reason that whole night.

I walk in and feel eerie, almost nauseas. I went upstairs and heard an odd noise. I grabbed my gun, which was always loaded. What was the point of having a gun if they can hear you loading it? I went into Tiffany and my room and seen a dark figure moving up and down on my bed.

I hit the light switch and seen a man who had robbed and was raping Tiffany. Her mouth was muffled. I shot him in the side and put him on the ground. I kick his wound and shoot him in his dick and then kicked it. I loved Tiffany and could not bear to see the look on her face, like she would never forget this and how could she. I made the man suffer as I stood confused. I finally shot the man in the face. The court said it was beyond self defense.

I looked at Tiffany and told her how sorry I was. "I promise I'll take this pain away from you, I'll put all the bad memories and pain on my back. I'll free you from this pain. I can't stand to see you so upset. I love you," and then I shot her in the head. Quick and painless then what she had just endured. I didn't want her to have to live with the thought, so I put her to rest in a better place, a place I wanted to be. I knew what would happen, the outcome. I never lied and never expected pity, or people to understand, but I knew I was doing her a favor. I looked into her eye's and I could swear I seen her shake her head yes. I loved her, she loved me. She would have done the same for me.

                    I made a point
                   To burn all the
                      Photographs

Woke up this morning, I didn't want to go
Didn't know where, I really didn't care
Work I guess, I'll get dressed
Smoke all of my anger all away,
But I knew it could never be true, always
alone, always with me,
But I know this is just a passing of time,
Trying to fight for my mind,
But I'm always out the door,
Searching for something, just a little more
Because I bought a lie, told you it's true
Never cared, just want to fuck you
Go or stay, either which way
I'll be gone starting today,
Sorry I never cared, sorry my mind will
never be there

Needle and a spoon

My back is killing me as I stand up from the floor. I look around and recognize only a couple of people. It's quiet, quiet like a morgue. I see dried blood in the ditch of my left arm. I wade through the trash and bodies hoping all of them are breathing. "Wake up, wake the fuck up," I start yelling to the nameless faces.

The strangers look up at me with anger. They begin to stand up and head for the door, some scratching their skin like it hurt them. I hear one girl puking outside as I head for my bedroom. "Are you okay?" She looks up at me saying nothing. The cars were cleared out and it seemed as if she was left behind.

"Would you like to come in and sit down?" She still said nothing as she headed towards me. "There is the bathroom in my room." She goes in there and she asks if she could use my mouth wash. She was beautiful and her name was Brandy. Brandy came back into the living room and asked if she could have one of my cigarettes. "I see you have the same problem that I have. It's a rough lifestyle, how did a woman like you end up like me, if you don't mind me asking?

"Well Mike, I was going to school in Dallas. I went to a party and met a girl that lived over in the west side of Fort Worth. Everything was going good. I only smoked weed and attended school like I was suppose to and my grades never failed me. I and my new friend moved in together and that's when it went downhill. I didn't realize that my roommate was immature, young, a life not lived yet."

"So you move in and she brought you down. I mean we can never blame anybody but ourselves, but I understand what you mean." "She exposed me to a lot of bad things too quick." I was cooking up some dope as we talked, getting ready to roll a bowl. "Brandy you seem smarter than that. Me I'm destined to be a fuck up. "The funny thing Mike is I was the top of my class and a cheerleader, the whole nine yards in high school." "Well I wasn't expecting that."

Brandy and I shot up and she would lie on my couch and I lay on the floor, both of us just talking, going in and out of reality. "Brandy you should stop. I know that makes me a huge hypocrite, but you should get out while you can." "I'm not sure I want to be clean Mike and I'm not sure why that is."

Brandy and I became really good friends and I encouraged her to attend school during the week. I would even go to Dallas and stay a few nights to keep her grounded to reality. We became lovers quickly and this didn't help our addiction, her addiction. Brandy couldn't see me shoot up and not start to itch. There was that and then there was the simple pleasure of fucking after we got off and then got off again on that smack. Shit got serious when I did too much of some stronger H and I almost overdosed and died.

I moved back to my place in Fort Worth. Brandy came by a lot and I miss those nights together, wanting to make each night, each weekend last forever. Then I had to do what needed to be done. "Hey Brandy I know we are fucked up right now, but I don't want you to come around anymore. It's not right,

I'm a bad person and I don't want you around here anymore." "Mike you are a hypocrite." I was. "Why don't you practice what you preach, asshole? If you want to get rid of me to fuck one of your whores, than just say it, I don't deserve to be treated this way." "Please try and understand this from my side. I just don't think you should waste your time on me or this anymore. I have destroyed one life; I don't want to destroy two, even as much as I love you." "Fuck your, "LOVE," I don't buy that bullshit anymore. All those nights that you told me that me staring in your eye's drove you crazy and then you throw me away like a lump of shit. Well fuck you then Mike, you fucking man whore."

I understood why she was mad, but talking to her wouldn't have gotten through to her. I had to be drastic and firm. I told her that I wanted to kiss her, smell her, and see her beautiful eye's looking in mine, but I have to sacrifice for her life, not mine. "Let me just gather my things and I will be out of your fucking way." I didn't answer back; I thought it would be best anyway. I was the needle in her spoon

and she didn't need to be holding that
spoon anymore.

New song

It's one of the greatest feelings
in the world. There are no disputes on
the well known great feelings, sex,
etc.

Playing guitar is a reward on its
own, euphoric. When you write a new
song or riff you feel like you've
created real art, passion. It's a great
feeling, feeling like you've created
something like passion, love, hatred.
It's hard to come across that anymore.
We fuck, we disrespect, we hate each
other's ideas, we either get high or we
don't, we fuck up each other's lives,
or we hide. Sappy songs, plagues we are
unable to get the fuck away from. Some
old lives not letting new beginnings.

As an artist all that goes away
with the creation of art, even if it's
a book with a shitty ending, a short
chapter with someone not real, but not
you're song, my song. No your song is
forever yours, whether anybody likes
your creation or not. Somebody will
eventually see the same.

I had no intentions of living this way

At the age of 27 years old, I had no intentions of living this way, this state of mind. Life was innocent; it was carefree, never knowing where I would end up next. I believe everybody misses those days. Those young years, never sitting at home, only coming in to get a drink of water. My friends and I at those ages never knew we were poor. Money never crossed our young minds. None of us knew that money made and destroyed lives, family's. For us though money never played a role for us.

It would be many years later until we would discover the impact money had on the world. I remember going across the road and smashing quarters on the train tracks. The point is, we never thought of money, we were happy with the simple things in life. I wish I knew how to get back to that mentality, that feeling not to worry about living cost. People have always said that money can't buy you happiness. I have always wanted to say to the mouth saying this, to shut the fuck up. I would rather be depressed and have money, than to be poor and depressed. How did this happen? We can all pinpoint our turning point in life, but still, how did this happen?

At least with money you can pay a whore to take it in the ass. I had no intentions of living this way, but I do anyway.

Paper Towel

Paper towel, please wipe it all away.

No thought's, just shame, I wished I
knew her name.

I spilt my beer as you talked shit
through my ear. An ear so afraid to
listen, afraid to know what is being
said.

All this shame and guilt like love and
hate.

Sometimes we feel happy, sometimes sad,
but we make each other mad.

I wish I could wipe it all away.
Everything I had but couldn't keep.

I just wish I could wipe it all away.
Stranger's is what I see in an impure
world.

I wish I could just wipe it all away.
I wish she could wipe it all away.

Who is she? Too many common whores tame
the tiger by the tail.

I was interested in something on the
level.

Maybe I'm better without.

Just give me a clean slate, that first
day of sobriety that's all I ask in
this plea of sanity.

Porch

Haus and I sit and drink countless beers and bullshit. Sometimes I play guitar, sometimes we listen to great music on the record player, and sometimes the dogs just run around. Yeah there is air conditioning inside, TV, comfortable furniture, but were okay out here where we belong. We have a little radio going, or I just play guitar. I say that again because that was all we needed to laugh and have a good time. We light up joint after joint, open beer after beer, song after song. It's true we don't get to front porch lounge as much since a couple of years have passed, but I remember how it use to be. Were not simple people, just enjoying simple things. I have a hard time doing this naturally, but the front porch is a different story and having a true friend to drink with. I think it is just another reason to get out of the house, but rain or shine; it always turns out to be a good time, simple.

Simplicity is needed whether you are two years old or seventy six. When you lose your smile for some of these moments then you start to die. Everybody needs their own porch.

Rejection

I look at this pile of papers in front
of me. There are a lot of stories and poems
in there and mixed in the pile is rejection
letters. Rejection letters from publishers
and from crazy women. The women pile stings
worse than the publisher pile, fucking
women.

I look at this pile and it makes me
happy, never lowering my character. No, I
look and laugh, reading a little bit of
everything. The writing is terrible in sober
lighting. I feel a bit honored when I come
across a review of my work. That lets me
know somebody took the time to read
something I wrote. I'm no Hemingway; I am a
simple man and simple writings. I never took
a class, or was given advice, just my
passion for writing. There is no method to
my madness, just thought experiments.

Maybe someday I'll get a letter in the
mail that I could frame up, that I can show
off. There's nothing that set's me apart, I
just like doing what I do.

Black Heart

I walk down to the local tavern and all I hear is, "hey Mike how you today?" As I walk in I wave hello, my notebook in hand and the girl serving drinks knows what to bring to me. I'm not sure if it's sad that these people know me to well, or if I am picking at nothing?

I like to people watch and listen, not to be nosy just to hear the loud chatter with loose tongues as the people drink more. Most of the people are miserable though, sitting there every day as soon as the tavern opens up, but then again what am I doing here? I guess that's another fucked up question to be answered at another time. I drink listening to all the regulars as they tell such bitter stories. It's like they have given up on life a long time ago. Maybe life had given up on them?

I listen and write about things around me and things out of touch from true reality. I'm surrounded by black souls, black hearts, long faded, long pushed away.

I start to notice that I am surrounded by lost souls that will never return to a normal state of reasoning. I gave up on working, but I never thought I would slip into this type of life. I walk away; I walk home feeling sad, sad for what I have become, what I might become. The walk home had made me realize what I am and what I wasn't. I was a disowned child, a fuck up and tried to escape to see what I could find, but all I found was a lost black heart, a wondering soul.

Shameless self promoter

I'm guessing that there are thousands of writers in this world. I'm sure the majority of these writers have never had anything read by another set of eyes. That's a downer for a man like me, who loves to write. My writings are full of typos, miss-phrased sentences. They are sad, lonely, and full of life, passionate, selfish, and hateful and everything in between.

I stay optimistic though. I refuse to accept the facts of my present life. I refuse to stop here and become contempt. That's your life not mine, not my decision. What would I say if somebody asked me about my writings? Would they think that they know me? Would they judge me based on my mind wondering? Like I said though, I stay optimistic.

So I hand out cards, I speak into open ears, run ad's and sending in multiple copies to publishers. I wonder

if one will ever read a story, if one
will ever take a chance on me. I just
want to quit hating everyday life. I
would to love to be doing these things
that people never even think about.
I'm sure with my luck that somebody
might like me when I'm gone, turned to
ash. For now I will just be the
shameless self promoter, fingers
crossed

Shove it?

I stand here swinging a sledge hammer
as sweat stings my eyes. I think of how I
could have gone to college, what would I
have done then if I would have taken that
road all the way? I get a frantic call from
my boss, bitching at me for something I'm
not really sure about. I ignore and turn the
radio up, pick up the sledge and get back to
business. It's hard work being an iron
worker, heavy manual labor. These people
don't appreciate, or even humor me with
respect.

I make them their money though, because
as much as I hate that thought, I have to
except it, I need my cut. This is the monkey
on my back. Hating what you do is a terrible
thing. A person should enjoy what they spend
their time doing. You become bitter, it
becomes harder to wake up and go to work.
There has to be somebody who would like my
job. It's a great job that will actually
make a man feel good and accomplished at the
end of the day; I have just played out this
part, whatever that may be. It's all to
cookie cutter for me. I need scenery to
change, faces to change, life to change

I make them their money though, because
they have that same hold over me. I make it
for them so I can get my piece of cheese, so
I can make it another month. Wouldn't we all
just love to frolic in happiness, or to have
a little power for once? Life isn't done

with me yet, so I make my next move and life will make its and maybe one day, maybe, I'll beat life. Until that day comes, I will stick out this rat race, this insult to my life, just wishing I could look at the faces and tell them to shove it. That's not the way they want it, so that's not the way they're going to get it. I will just have to find a way around them all. Around what they want back to what I need.

Paris, I'm Sorry

I remember running through the metro in Paris. My friends and I were trying to make it to the train on time to head to Amsterdam. The night before was our first day in Paris and like always, or any situation for that matter, we were always out on the town. I immediately split from my friends to get as much of the nightlife in that I could. Not nightclub nightlife, but the underground part of Paris.

It's always a beautiful city, but this night was pure adrenaline. I hit every little dive like I'm in Texas and taking in every wonder in that late night, early morning hours. The red light district was busy and pitiful. I love to sit back and watch people, but these were the type people who were shady in every way, even in their eyes. I continue to hit the little dives, that don't even have signs and stay to myself. I did meet an American woman, but what was the fun in that? It would be wasted time, time I can spend in America wasting.

Life handed us an opportunity in life and I wanted to make the best. Finding women to fuck was the easy part. "Mike this dude has some weed at his flat. We are going to with him for a bit." That was actually perfect. I could see more and do more without them to slow me down. I was wanting to take in a lot more, so it was alright for

them to go run around to go find dirt weed
and I could continue my exploring. We met up
at the hotel and I wanted to keep drunk, so
that's what I did, alone. I could sleep on
the train; surrogate myself from their
childish antics.

Sunrise, Sunset

I feel like my head is stuck in the
clouds, like everything is fading to black.
Like I'm being pushed away and never want to
come back. What seems like yesterday was
actually a few years ago. That's fucked up
when I think about it, being able to say a
few years ago. This makes me mourn for
wasted time. The stuff I could have
achieved, learned, maybe different choices
and goals could have been made. Drinking
cheap beer, alone, thinking of all those
friends from my past. My first mistake in
this world was thinking I could relate. They
tell me it all comes together in relative
ways. Whatever the fuck that means.
Everybody has the answer, when they are just
as confused as me, but in denial.

I don't let the mourning for lost time
get me down. No this is more of a thought
for the moment. A person cannot live in the
past, but you can learn from it and I
believe this is okayed, not sad or painful.
Everything happens and changes so quickly,
it's sunrise, sunset. Is living for today,
wrong? Why should a person not go all out
every day of their alive? After all life is
quick and full of shame and regrets.
Sunrise, sunset. It's your conscience, or
maybe just mine?

Tell me when she's gone

I've been in Vegas for a week now. I left one night without telling anybody, not telling Tara. I'm a chicken shit like most people. I was hiding out in Las Vegas, hoping she would leave me.

My mind won't allow me to wonder, but I try. I order an escort and score an oz of cocaine. For four days I had no grip on reality. I need my friend to call and tell me she is gone. I'll die in Texas or Vegas this is certain, a thought out fate, a smile on my face.

Tara use to go to AA meetings with me, she also use to curl in my arms making me feel important, feeling like one person would show up to my day, my funeral. Those feelings were long gone though. Tara no longer cared.

I imagine she came home from work, stripping and found no sign of me. Sure I was just one of her filthy Johns, but she said she loved me.

This is a lonely day as I look at my pale skin, no meat on my bones. I still want to die, nobody knowing. I have nothing linking me to anybody, just a city full of sin. Maybe I could be saved if I got word that she was gone, but she has no ambition, no passion.

I lay out three rails as I look at the whore sleeping in my bed. I was out of money and time. I rolled a twenty dollar bill and snort the rails. I guess I thought I could head out to leave it all behind. I have a moment of weakness and call a friend. Nobody knew I was gone, so I lead them to believe I was home. She will never be gone, physically and mentally.

I feel deaths cold grip as I take the whores money as she sleeps and leave for darkness of the streets. I leave with nothing but a backpack and a broken afternoon. I walk in the dark, yet lit up sky line. I buy some more coke and snort it up before catching the cab. I purchased a ticket to Bosnia. I pop my little white pills, my body trying to reject them, but I won't let it. I damn near overdose on the plane, after leaving the runway, nobody paying attention obviously. My bad luck pulls me through the easiest overdose, if you can call it that.

I knew Bosnia was beautiful, like the women and the drugs were cheap. I land and stumble of the plane looking like a skeleton. Life no longer appealed to me, was I alive? Tara would never be gone, not matter what. I head for the rough part and score some smack. I paid cash for a shitty room, soon to be my sanctuary. I go out after rigging up and find the perfect whore. I fuck her all night as we shot smack up all through that dark night. "Where are you Tara?" I wake up and the whore was dead, heart failure I imagine, so lucky. I leave her and hit the streets finding a phone.

"By Tara." I said I wouldn't call, but luck sent me to her voicemail. I scored enough. I found refuge in a nearby train yard. I climb into an empty train car and lay down for a minute, I was tired. I found my spot, my place. A country that would throw me in a field dead that nobody would find me. They will check my pockets and toss me never to be found. I see the blood mix with the cooked up smack and slowly drain into my lifeless body. It didn't matter where I went I wouldn't be able

to escape myself. I remember these
final moments. I remember thinking
there was no need for a suicide note,
so I do it. I wrote this story, but not
for a cry for help.

Time bomb

It was dumb how exciting it would be with young love. Naomi had me captivated. She was gorgeous, no questions about that, she was better looking than me. Naomi seemed to like me though and I thought about her all the time. I actually couldn't stand to be away from her, it goes to show you how young I was.

We were young, so naturally I was always trying to get her away from her family and her house. I remember how we were really happy to see each other. The day's I didn't get to see her, I would write letter's and wonder what she was doing. I remember our first spring break how excited I was that I was able to see her three days in a row. Naomi was a virgin and I was a ticking time bomb. She was half good girl, and had a little bad girl in her to. I tried hard to bring out the bad in her. We loved each other, but both of us hated to love.

As we grew older, we had a on and off again relationship. I would fuck whatever I could when she would break up with me and then I would convince myself that I missed her. I was so fucked up that I never knew, I don't believe I really cared. Naomi grew in a different direction, but I always remember taking our close off in dark places, not caring. I don't want to hear from her, or about her, but I wish her well. I remember placing my fingers in her notches up and down her spine. I will take her though and leave her alone.

Too much not to be doing

A world full of so much energy, yet confusion, so many different things to consume over a short lifetime. I try to accomplish or attempt certain activities, but I don't. It's not because I don't want to, it's just all so overwhelming. Too much puts me into a rat hole. There's a story that could be wrote, women to be fucked, songs to be wrote, yards to mow, people to call, work and that's just the tip of the cold ass iceberg.

Do some people ever accomplish even a third that they ever attempt to do? I get overwhelmed by a handful of task let alone a full schedule. There is just too much not to be doing. I'll never write the great novel, or collection, no unforgettable song, or a woman who adores my everything, my dick. I'll just sit alone, drinking, wondering what I could have done with what talents I held at certain times. I realize that my lack of doing was me not wanting to do. There is just too much not to be doing.

You're so fucking
Special

There never seemed to be a pleasant
moment with you. Never a fuck at sunset,
never a worry free night. Even laying with
you was unpleasant. She was always
complaining, complaining over stuff that had
nothing to do with her. Something had turned
her bitter; every word she spoke was
hateful. Her friends, family, random people,
she would bitch about everything. The only
thing I could tell about her that was
special was the fact that she was a good
lay, but cold afterwards.

I asked her how this was all relative
to life. Wasting time on nothing, always
missing the point, pointing your fingers at
me. When she broke things off with me, she
did it in a vulgar display of power; I wish
I could have put a curse on her. What made
her so fucking special? What made me or
anybody, anything for that matter? What gave
some people the right to live easily and
other's always battling up hill, stuck under
somebody's thumb. Who decided this, TV? The
magazines? When did the masses begin to
think they were so fucking special? I had to
ask myself what I had become, if I was
really living, or just breathing, blood
pumping. Who had I become? Had I grew numb
toward these attention getting whores we
call celebrities, the rich, the powers to
be? I may have grown numb, but I can't help

but wonder what makes these people so
fucking special

Worst cup of coffee

I had stopped in for a quick bite to eat and to get off the road for a bit. I had been on the road for five hours straight and needed to stretch my legs. It was 7a.m., I had decided to load my guitar up and find some place to hide out for a few days. My house was getting to me, too much time in there writing, drinking, and smoking too many cigarettes. Life was going good, but I feared I was going crazy. I grabbed some weed and pills and a few clothes and took off down the road.

Then after five hours into the night I stop in at a breakfast house, to grab some coffee and pancakes. They set me next to three middle aged men, one whom couldn't stop starring at me, so I made him feel uncomfortable. The nice waitress with too much makeup and perfume brings my pancakes out and also the food to the three guys next to me. I almost want to tell the lady if she toned down the look a bit she wouldn't be that bad, but I sit there eating, sucking down the coffee. The three men were talking and talking about fucking golf.

I had stopped in and was having a rare moment where my mind was at a standstill. I was trying hard not to think about my Faith. I'm an innocent bystander and over hear all their bullshit. After about thirty minutes, I tip the lady and pay the bill; I take one

last drink of bad coffee for the road and
head out. I get in the truck and put my
safety belt on. I get down the road,
listening to my favorite rock band and I
start to wonder. I wonder why I had to sit
through all that shit they were talking,
when I was supposed to be out of earshot,
but they were loud and excited. I guess it
was their day. They were on a play date.

You are free my precious thing

How much time must a man write of his dark and lonely times?

She was here, but I had no idea,

Now I feel that ironic feeling slipping over me,

Something wrote errantly, something to remind me.

Will she come back to save me? Or will she choose to be free?

She is my precious thing, never knew what to say, and ashamed of my ways, but this is the last time though, for me, my very soul.

For her life, I couldn't give a fuck.

Maybe my life is the precious thing?

You won't have to worry about me calling back west my sweet thing.

Does he know? Does he know all the great things that I knew but ignored?

But I'm a man and I'm aloud to do and think as I want to, get that straight.

You got that right? I could eat you alive.

That precious thing is my heart. Don't forget that and you won't.

You got that right? I just want to look at you all day, there isn't nothing wrong with that. There is nothing that could wash you away.

Clear Visions

I close my eyes and let it all slip
away,
The drugs help, but they can't take it all
away.
I see so clearly, what I could not see
before,
I was blind to your lies, Can't fool me
anymore
You tried to change what you could not
see,
What you can't control, I was blind to your
lies.
There was no mistake, just cruel
reality,
Like working while the sun sets, death
during birth.
I'm not blind anymore, choosing not to
look,
You can't exists if I can't see you

About the author

Marshall Sanders was born in Fort Worth Texas in August 1981. His passion for writing and music has helped contribute to his other passion of traveling. Marshall writes of the gritty underworld as he lives in it, in his moment. When Marshall isn't traveling, he spends his time writing with his dog Brewtus by his side and a guitar in arms reach. Living Life